Roba

Billy & Buddy

BORED SILLY WITH BILLY

9th CINEBOOK
The 9th Art Publisher

Original title: Boule & Bill 19 – Ras le Bill
Original edition: © Studio Boule & Bill, 2008
by Roba
English translation: © 2010 Cinebook Ltd
Translator: Luke Spear
Lettering and text layout: Imadjinn
This edition first published in Great Britain in 2010 by
Cinebook Ltd
56 Beech Avenue
Canterbury, Kent
CT4 7TA
www.cinebook.com
Second printing: February 2022
Printed in Spain by EGEDSA
A CIP catalogue record for this book
is available from the British Library
ISBN 978-1-84918-049-8

9th CINEBOOK
The 9th Art Publisher

Thieving Magpies

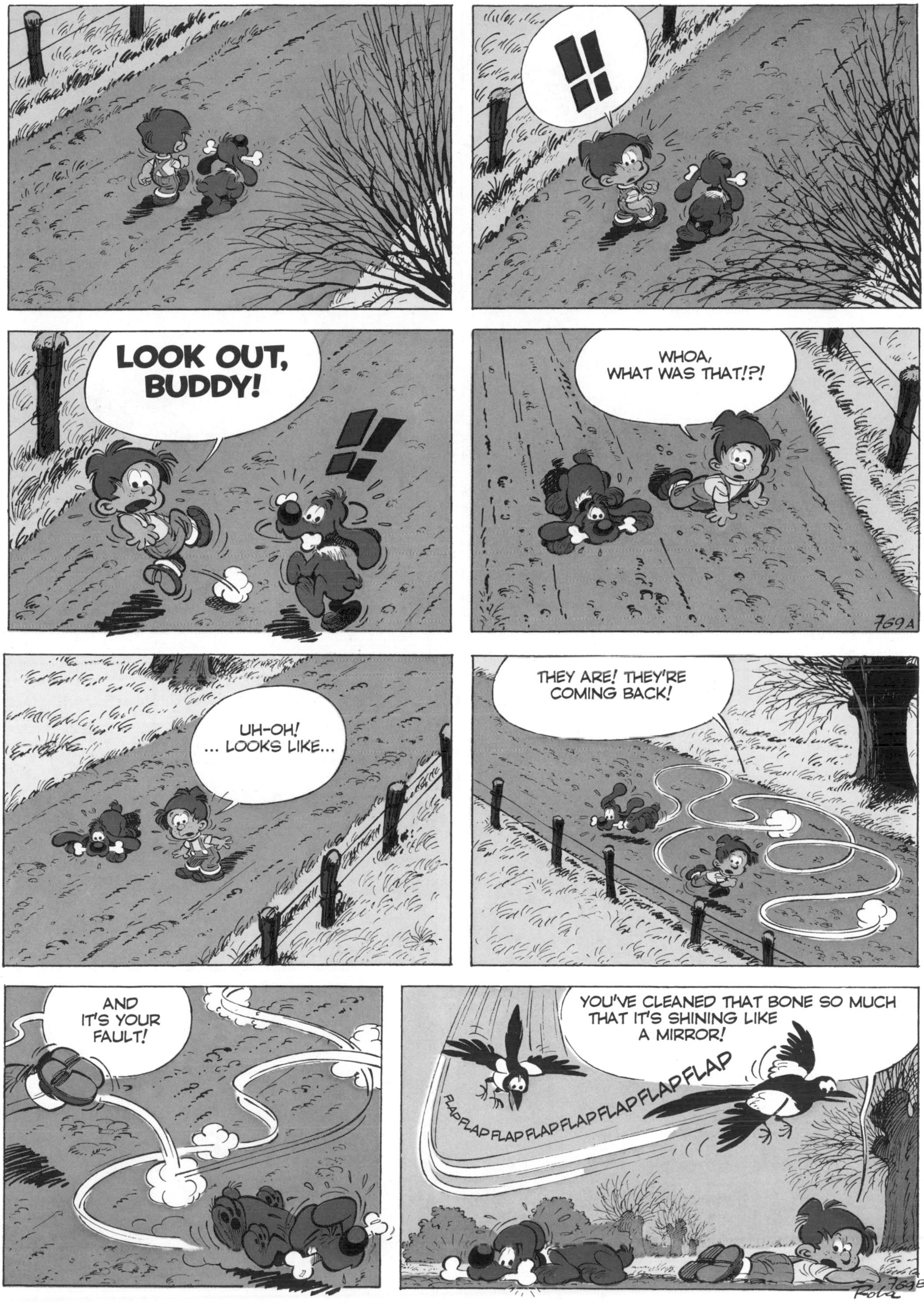

LOOK OUT, BUDDY!
WHOA, WHAT WAS THAT!?!
UH-OH! ... LOOKS LIKE...
THEY ARE! THEY'RE COMING BACK!
AND IT'S YOUR FAULT!
YOU'VE CLEANED THAT BONE SO MUCH THAT IT'S SHINING LIKE A MIRROR!
FLAP FLAP FLAP FLAP FLAP FLAP FLAP FLAP FLAP

He Who Plays with Stubble, Gets Prickled

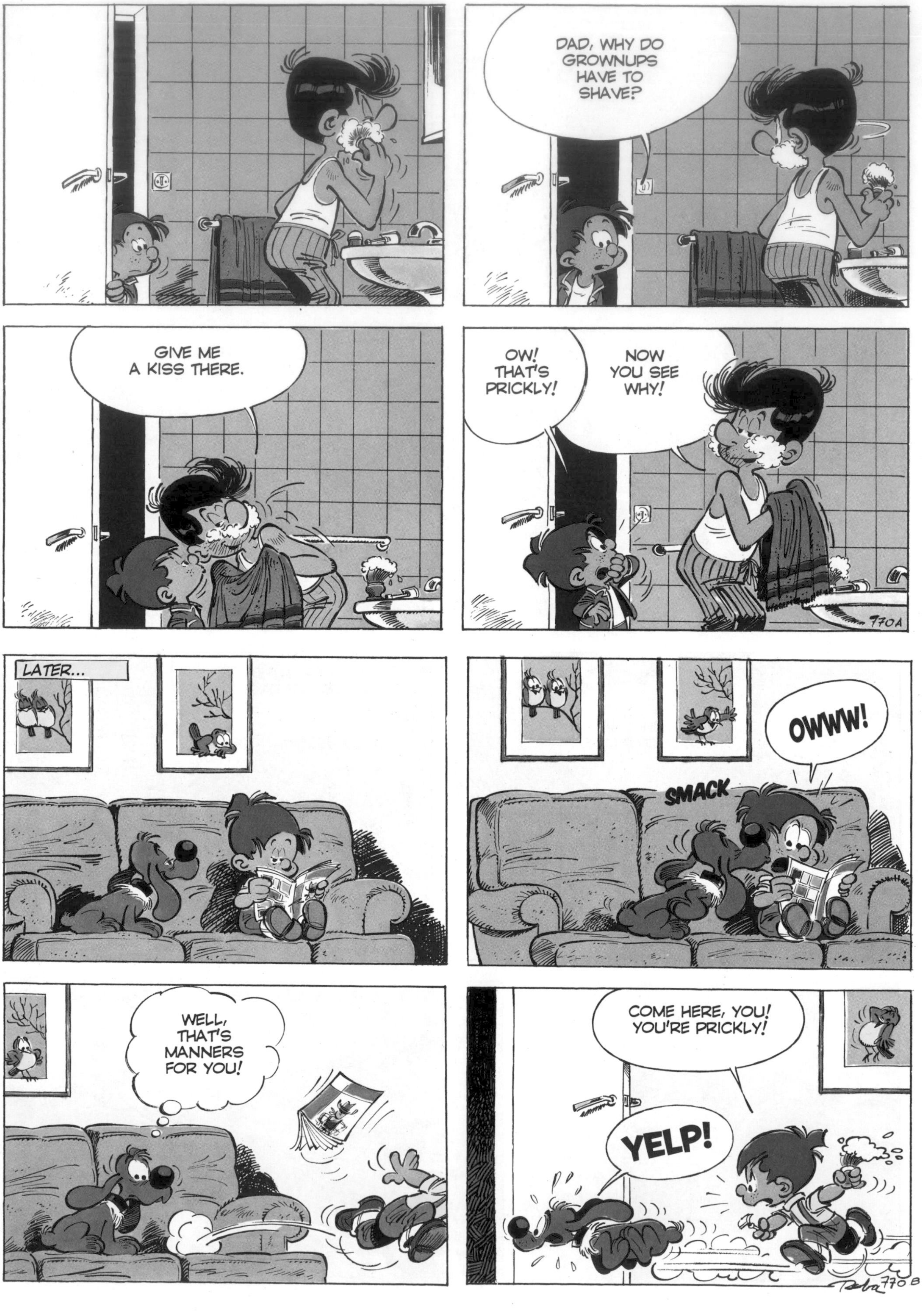
DAD, WHY DO GROWNUPS HAVE TO SHAVE?
GIVE ME A KISS THERE.
OW! THAT'S PRICKLY!
NOW YOU SEE WHY!
770A
LATER...
SMACK
OWWW!
WELL, THAT'S MANNERS FOR YOU!
COME HERE, YOU! YOU'RE PRICKLY!
YELP!
770B

One-upmanship

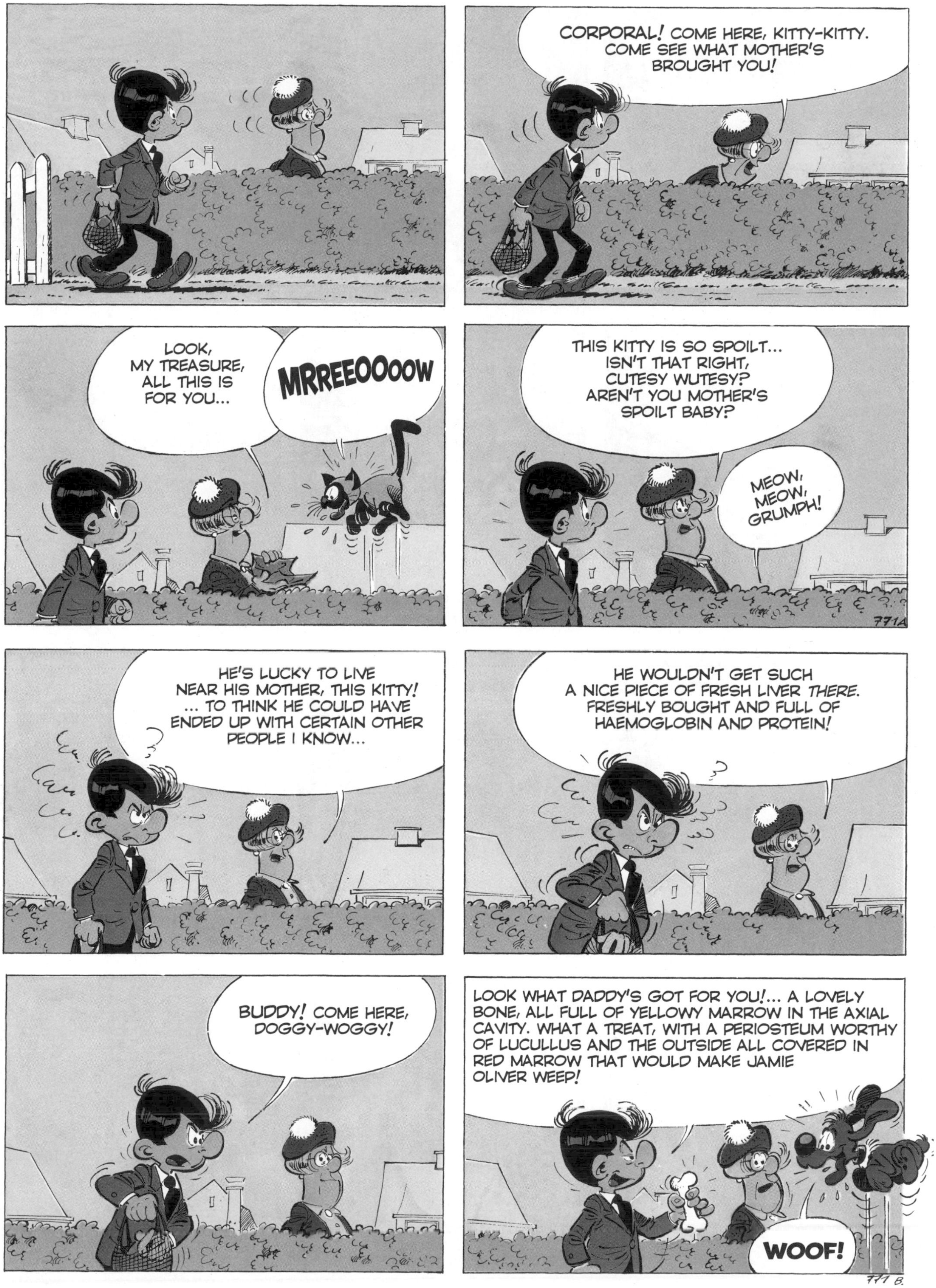

CORPORAL! COME HERE, KITTY-KITTY. COME SEE WHAT MOTHER'S BROUGHT YOU!
LOOK, MY TREASURE, ALL THIS IS FOR YOU...
MRREEOOOOW
THIS KITTY IS SO SPOILT... ISN'T THAT RIGHT, CUTESY WUTESY? AREN'T YOU MOTHER'S SPOILT BABY?
MEOW, MEOW, GRUMPH!
771A
HE'S LUCKY TO LIVE NEAR HIS MOTHER, THIS KITTY! ... TO THINK HE COULD HAVE ENDED UP WITH CERTAIN OTHER PEOPLE I KNOW...
HE WOULDN'T GET SUCH A NICE PIECE OF FRESH LIVER THERE. FRESHLY BOUGHT AND FULL OF HAEMOGLOBIN AND PROTEIN!
BUDDY! COME HERE, DOGGY-WOGGY!
LOOK WHAT DADDY'S GOT FOR YOU!... A LOVELY BONE, ALL FULL OF YELLOWY MARROW IN THE AXIAL CAVITY. WHAT A TREAT, WITH A PERIOSTEUM WORTHY OF LUCULLUS AND THE OUTSIDE ALL COVERED IN RED MARROW THAT WOULD MAKE JAMIE OLIVER WEEP!
WOOF!
771 B.

Top and Tail

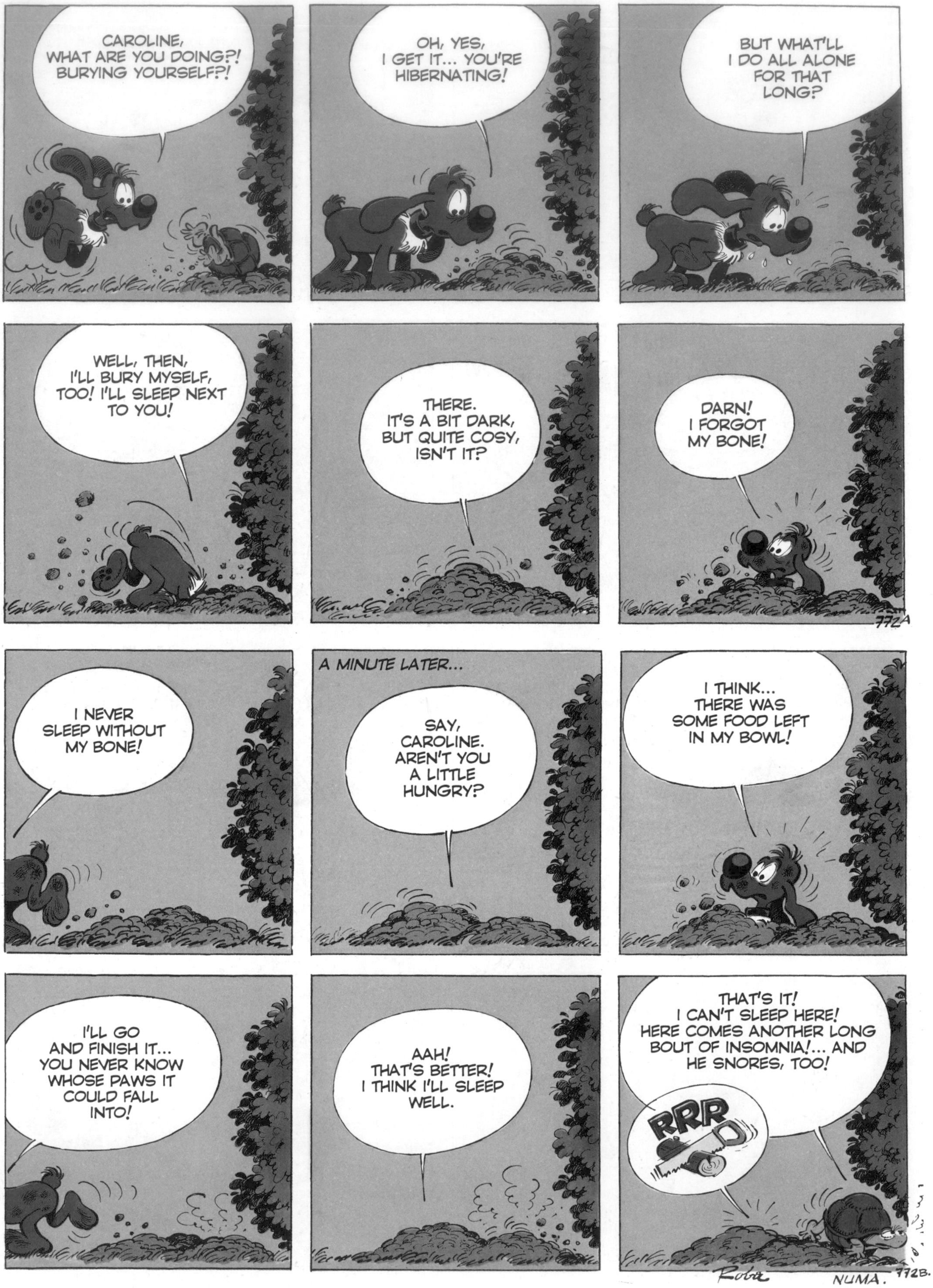
CAROLINE, WHAT ARE YOU DOING?! BURYING YOURSELF?!
OH, YES, I GET IT... YOU'RE HIBERNATING!
BUT WHAT'LL I DO ALL ALONE FOR THAT LONG?
WELL, THEN, I'LL BURY MYSELF, TOO! I'LL SLEEP NEXT TO YOU!
THERE. IT'S A BIT DARK, BUT QUITE COSY, ISN'T IT?
DARN! I FORGOT MY BONE!
772A
I NEVER SLEEP WITHOUT MY BONE!
A MINUTE LATER...
SAY, CAROLINE. AREN'T YOU A LITTLE HUNGRY?
I THINK... THERE WAS SOME FOOD LEFT IN MY BOWL!
I'LL GO AND FINISH IT... YOU NEVER KNOW WHOSE PAWS IT COULD FALL INTO!
AAH! THAT'S BETTER! I THINK I'LL SLEEP WELL.
THAT'S IT! I CAN'T SLEEP HERE! HERE COMES ANOTHER LONG BOUT OF INSOMNIA!... AND HE SNORES, TOO!
RRR
Roba
NUMA. 772B.

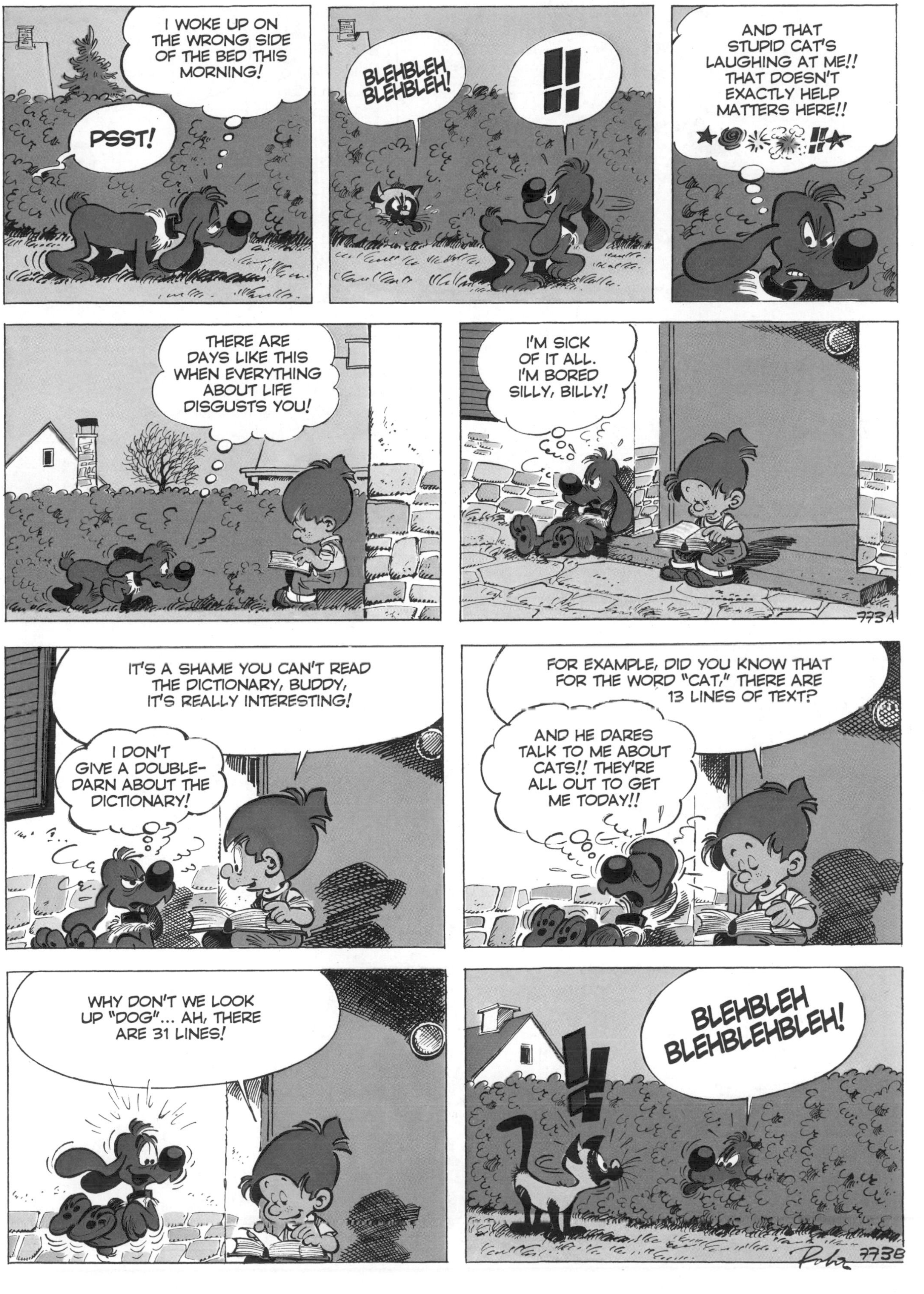
I WOKE UP ON THE WRONG SIDE OF THE BED THIS MORNING!
PSST!
BLEHBLEH BLEHBLEH!
!!
AND THAT STUPID CAT'S LAUGHING AT ME!! THAT DOESN'T EXACTLY HELP MATTERS HERE!!
THERE ARE DAYS LIKE THIS WHEN EVERYTHING ABOUT LIFE DISGUSTS YOU!
I'M SICK OF IT ALL. I'M BORED SILLY, BILLY!
773A
IT'S A SHAME YOU CAN'T READ THE DICTIONARY, BUDDY, IT'S REALLY INTERESTING!
I DON'T GIVE A DOUBLE-DARN ABOUT THE DICTIONARY!
FOR EXAMPLE, DID YOU KNOW THAT FOR THE WORD "CAT," THERE ARE 13 LINES OF TEXT?
AND HE DARES TALK TO ME ABOUT CATS!! THEY'RE ALL OUT TO GET ME TODAY!!
WHY DON'T WE LOOK UP "DOG"... AH, THERE ARE 31 LINES!
BLEHBLEH BLEHBLEHBLEH!
Roba
773B

The Butter Dish

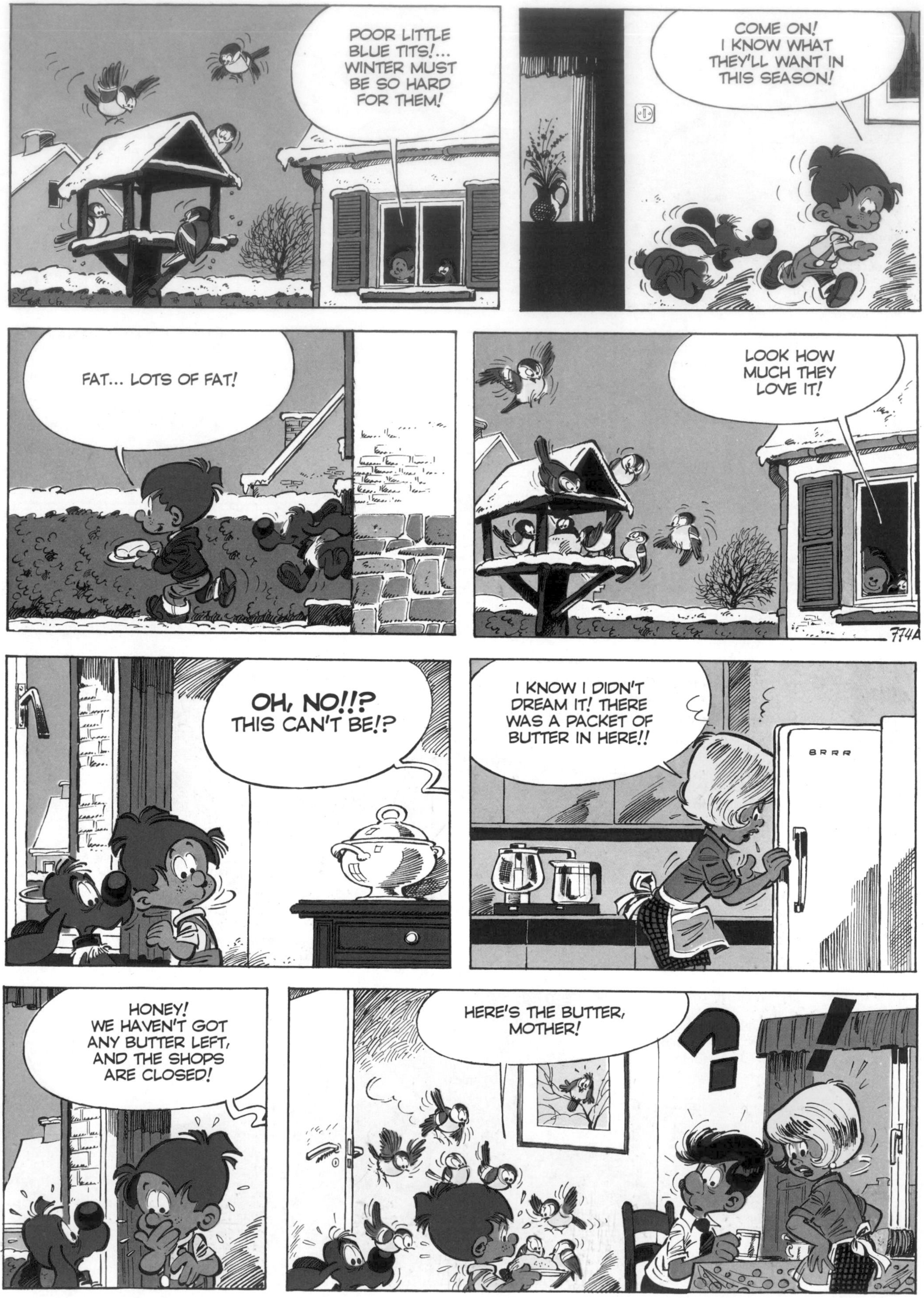
POOR LITTLE BLUE TITS!... WINTER MUST BE SO HARD FOR THEM!
COME ON! I KNOW WHAT THEY'LL WANT IN THIS SEASON!
FAT... LOTS OF FAT!
LOOK HOW MUCH THEY LOVE IT!
774A
OH, NO!!? THIS CAN'T BE!?
I KNOW I DIDN'T DREAM IT! THERE WAS A PACKET OF BUTTER IN HERE!!
BRRR
HONEY! WE HAVEN'T GOT ANY BUTTER LEFT, AND THE SHOPS ARE CLOSED!
HERE'S THE BUTTER, MOTHER!
?!

Photograwful!

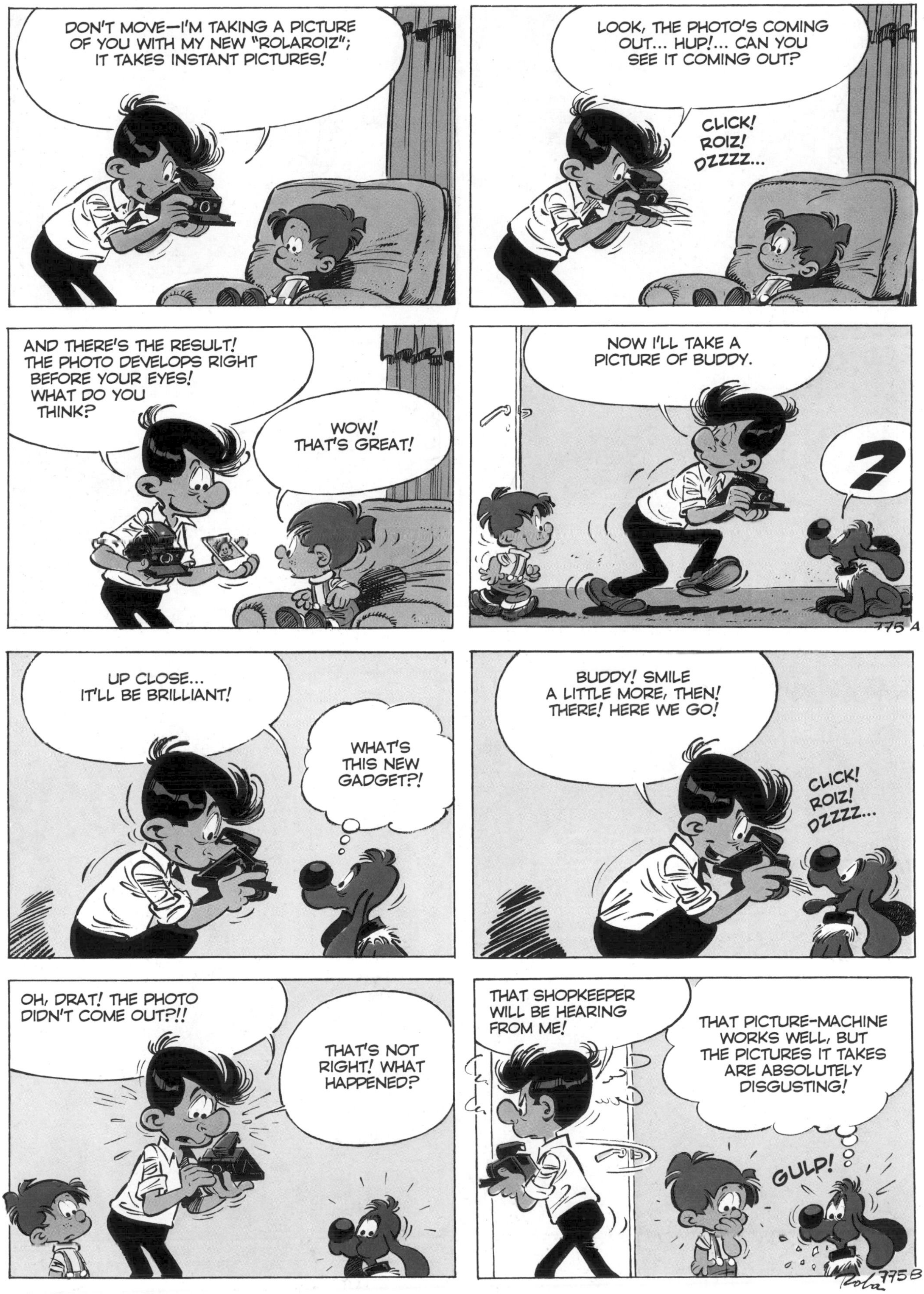
DON'T MOVE—I'M TAKING A PICTURE OF YOU WITH MY NEW "ROLAROIZ"; IT TAKES INSTANT PICTURES!
LOOK, THE PHOTO'S COMING OUT... HUP!... CAN YOU SEE IT COMING OUT?
CLICK! ROIZ! DZZZZ...
AND THERE'S THE RESULT! THE PHOTO DEVELOPS RIGHT BEFORE YOUR EYES! WHAT DO YOU THINK?
WOW! THAT'S GREAT!
NOW I'LL TAKE A PICTURE OF BUDDY.
?
775 A
UP CLOSE... IT'LL BE BRILLIANT!
WHAT'S THIS NEW GADGET?!
BUDDY! SMILE A LITTLE MORE, THEN! THERE! HERE WE GO!
CLICK! ROIZ! DZZZZ...
OH, DRAT! THE PHOTO DIDN'T COME OUT?!!
THAT'S NOT RIGHT! WHAT HAPPENED?
THAT SHOPKEEPER WILL BE HEARING FROM ME!
THAT PICTURE-MACHINE WORKS WELL, BUT THE PICTURES IT TAKES ARE ABSOLUTELY DISGUSTING!
GULP!
Roba 775 B

A Butchery

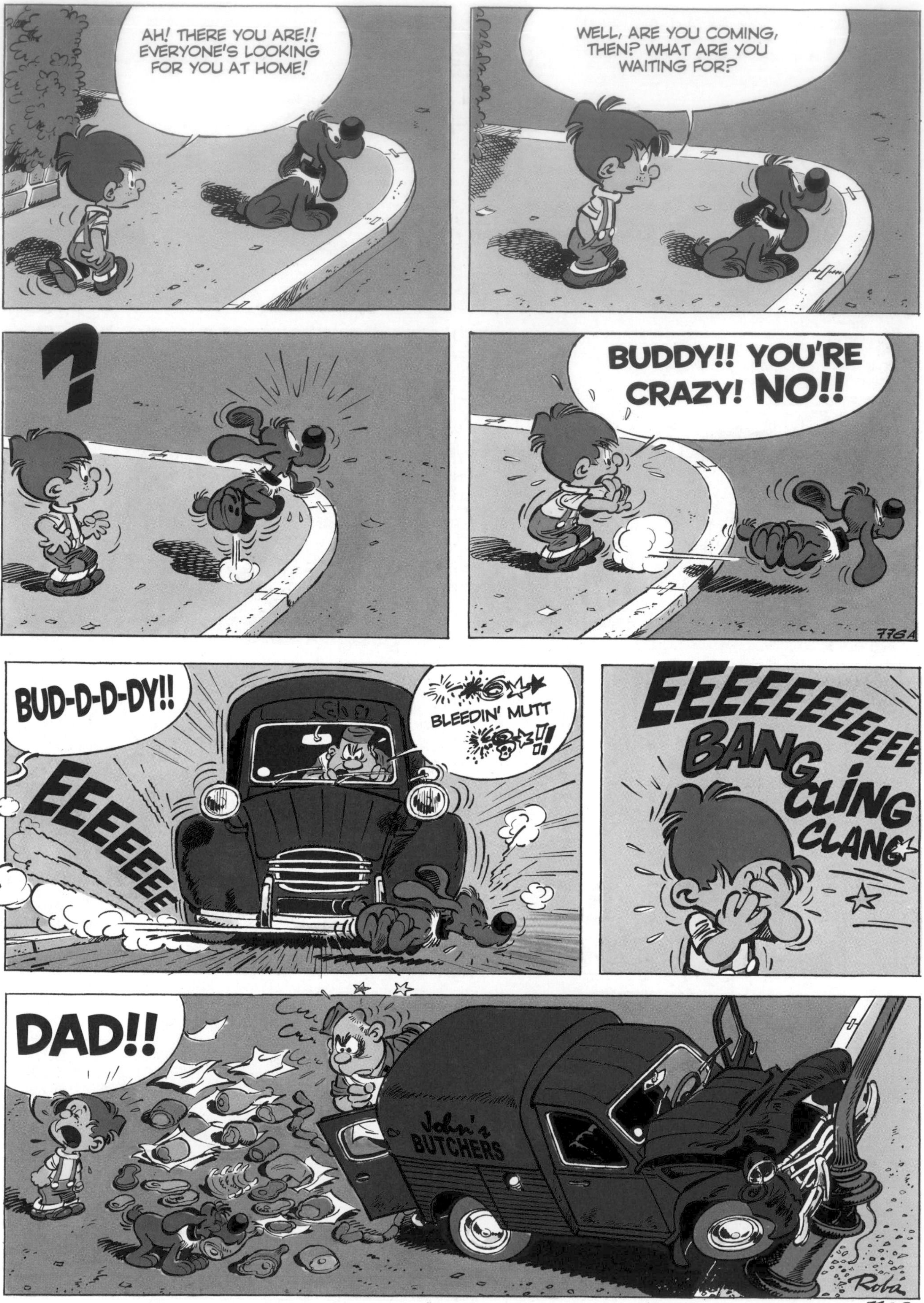
AH! THERE YOU ARE!! EVERYONE'S LOOKING FOR YOU AT HOME!
WELL, ARE YOU COMING, THEN? WHAT ARE YOU WAITING FOR?
?
BUDDY!! YOU'RE CRAZY! NO!!
776 A
BUD-D-D-DY!!
EEEEEEE
BLEEDIN' MUTT
EEEEEEEEEEE
BANG
CLING
CLANG
DAD!!
John's BUTCHERS
Roba
776 B.

Throw Me a Bone Here

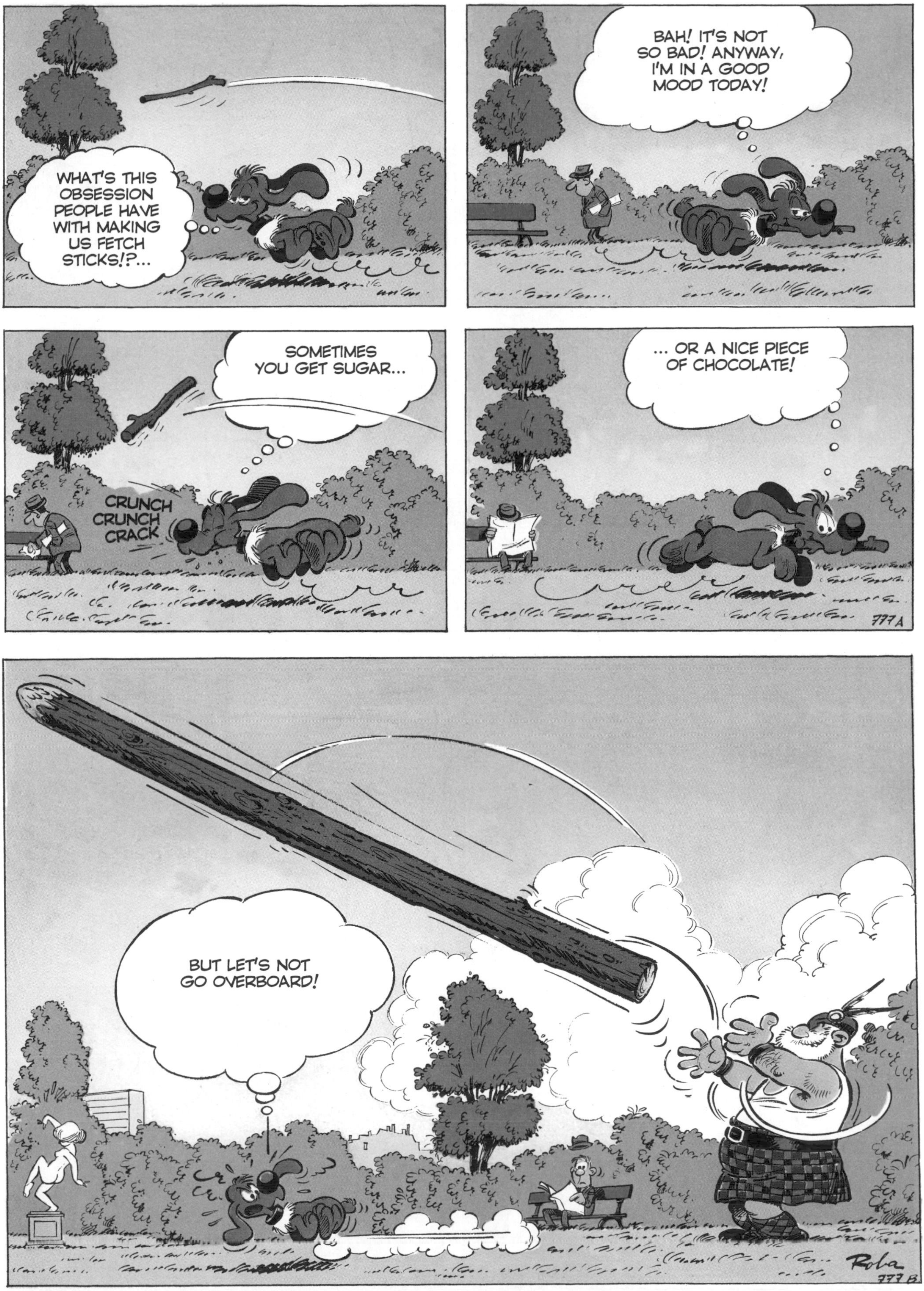
WHAT'S THIS OBSESSION PEOPLE HAVE WITH MAKING US FETCH STICKS!?...
BAH! IT'S NOT SO BAD! ANYWAY, I'M IN A GOOD MOOD TODAY!
SOMETIMES YOU GET SUGAR...
CRUNCH CRUNCH CRACK
... OR A NICE PIECE OF CHOCOLATE!
777A
BUT LET'S NOT GO OVERBOARD!
Roba
777B

Some Days You Just Can't Win...

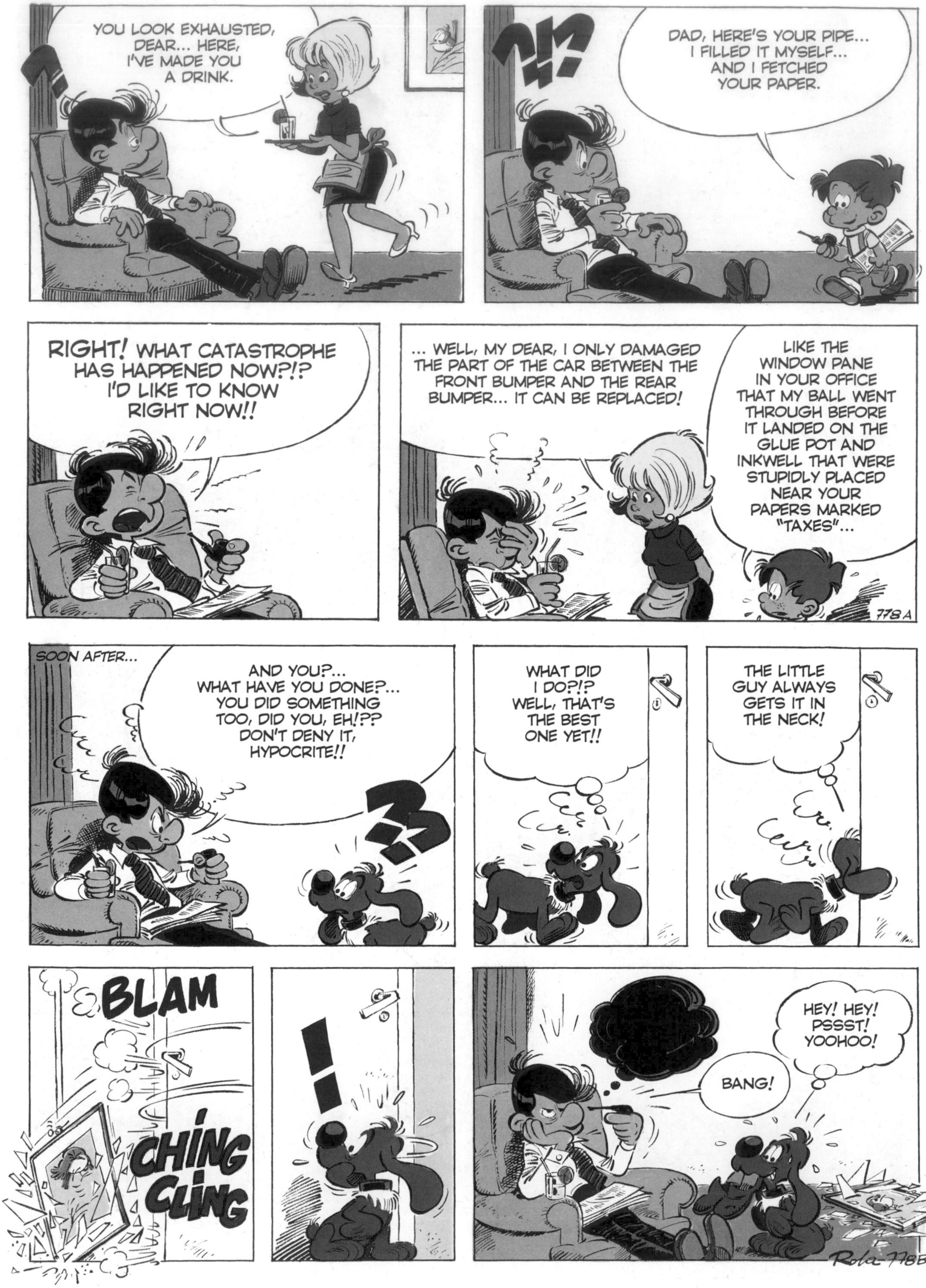

YOU LOOK EXHAUSTED, DEAR... HERE, I'VE MADE YOU A DRINK.
?!?
DAD, HERE'S YOUR PIPE... I FILLED IT MYSELF... AND I FETCHED YOUR PAPER.
RIGHT! WHAT CATASTROPHE HAS HAPPENED NOW?!? I'D LIKE TO KNOW RIGHT NOW!!
... WELL, MY DEAR, I ONLY DAMAGED THE PART OF THE CAR BETWEEN THE FRONT BUMPER AND THE REAR BUMPER... IT CAN BE REPLACED!
LIKE THE WINDOW PANE IN YOUR OFFICE THAT MY BALL WENT THROUGH BEFORE IT LANDED ON THE GLUE POT AND INKWELL THAT WERE STUPIDLY PLACED NEAR YOUR PAPERS MARKED "TAXES"...
778 A
SOON AFTER...
AND YOU?... WHAT HAVE YOU DONE?... YOU DID SOMETHING TOO, DID YOU, EH!?? DON'T DENY IT, HYPOCRITE!!
??
WHAT DID I DO?!? WELL, THAT'S THE BEST ONE YET!!
THE LITTLE GUY ALWAYS GETS IT IN THE NECK!
BLAM
CHING CLING
!!
BANG!
HEY! HEY! PSSST! YOOHOO!
Roba 778B.

Buddy and Bally

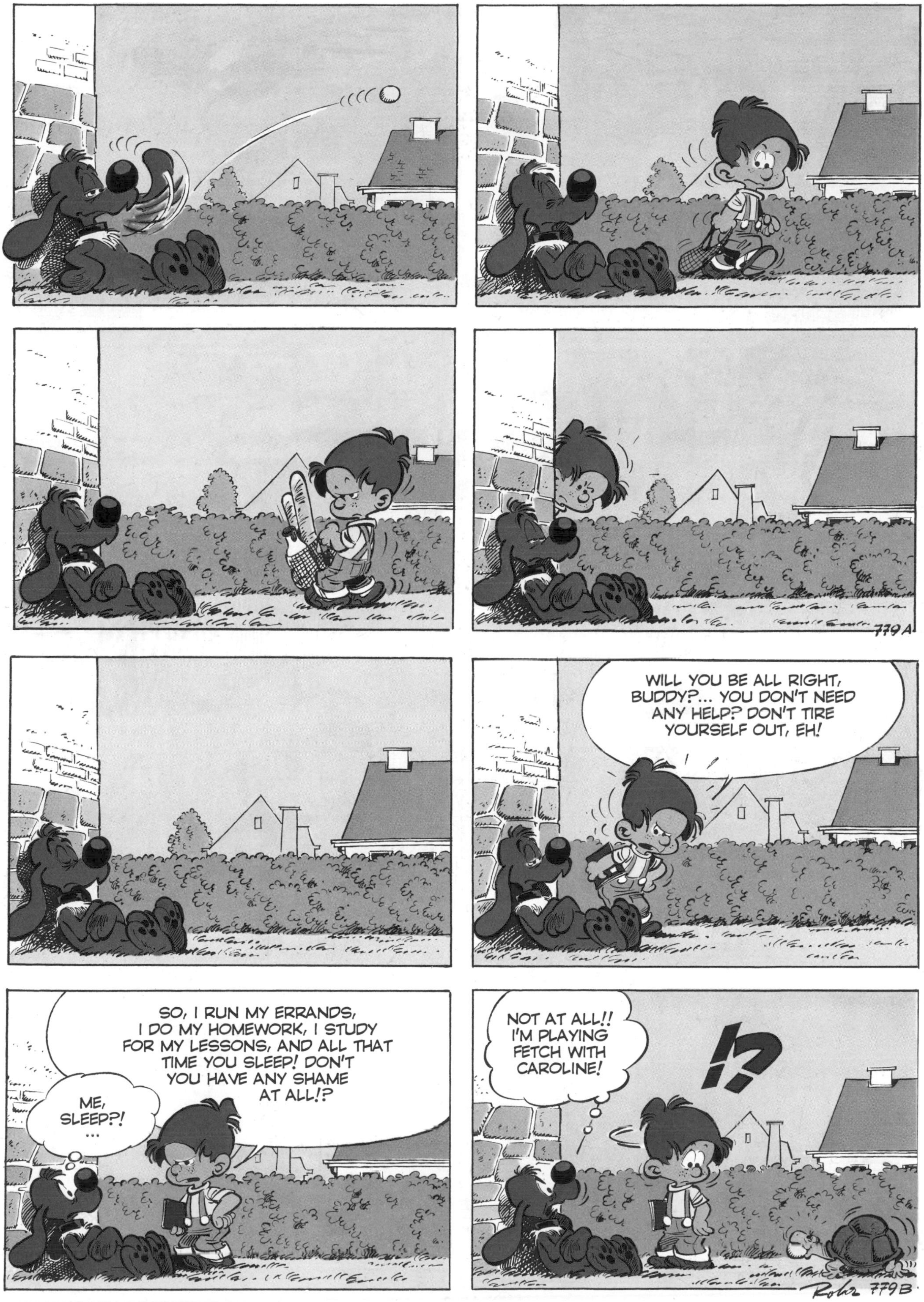

779 A
WILL YOU BE ALL RIGHT, BUDDY?... YOU DON'T NEED ANY HELP? DON'T TIRE YOURSELF OUT, EH!
SO, I RUN MY ERRANDS, I DO MY HOMEWORK, I STUDY FOR MY LESSONS, AND ALL THAT TIME YOU SLEEP! DON'T YOU HAVE ANY SHAME AT ALL!?
ME, SLEEP?! ...
NOT AT ALL!! I'M PLAYING FETCH WITH CAROLINE!
!?
Roba 779 B

Off the Scale

780A
OH!
I'VE PUT ON 40 POUNDS!!!
HEE, HEE! HEE, HEE!
40 POUNDS?!
BOOHOO!
BOOHOOOO!
780B

Tough Times Call for Tougher Fathers

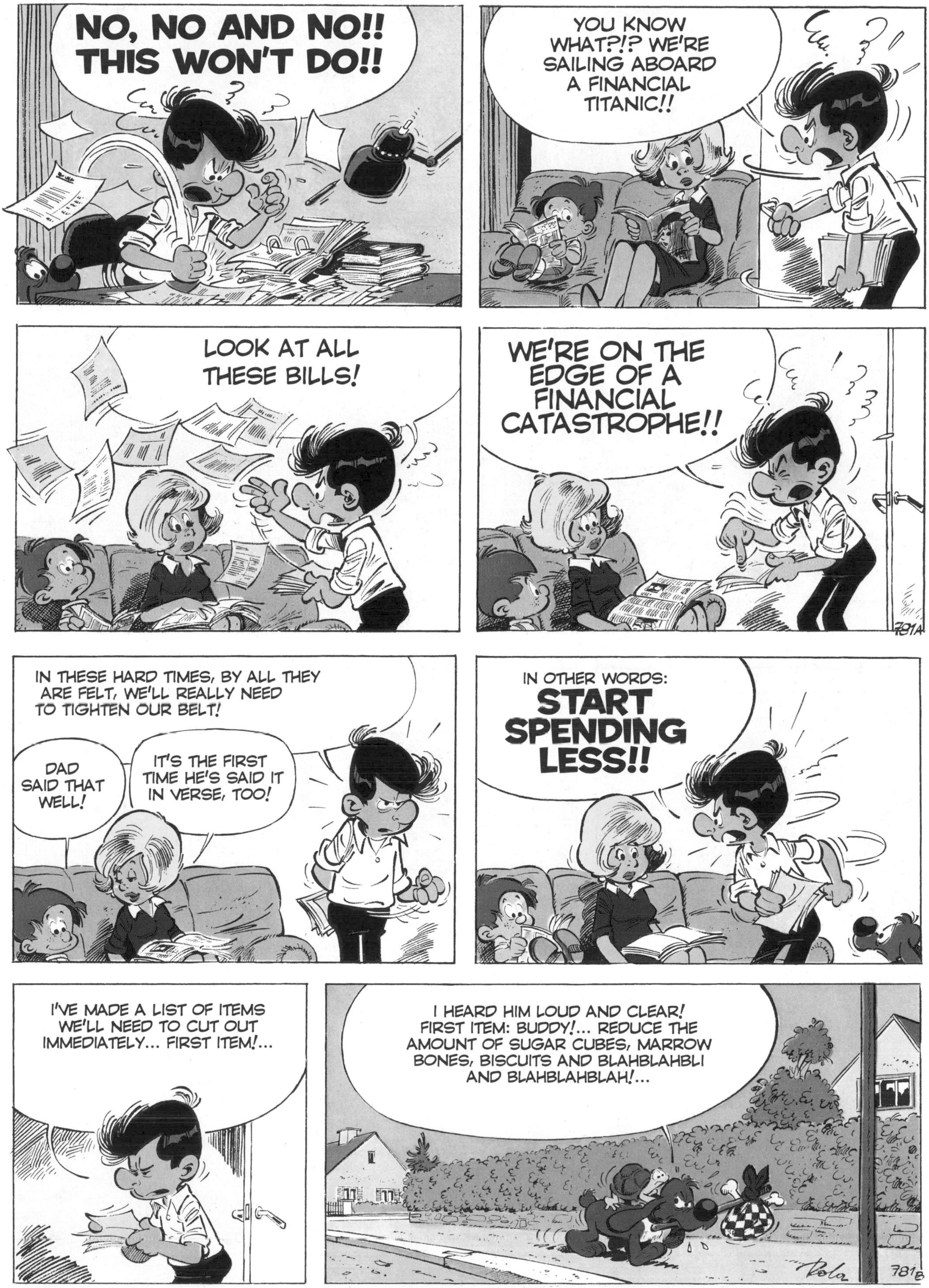
NO, NO AND NO!! THIS WON'T DO!!
YOU KNOW WHAT?!? WE'RE SAILING ABOARD A FINANCIAL TITANIC!!
LOOK AT ALL THESE BILLS!
WE'RE ON THE EDGE OF A FINANCIAL CATASTROPHE!!
IN THESE HARD TIMES, BY ALL THEY ARE FELT, WE'LL REALLY NEED TO TIGHTEN OUR BELT!
DAD SAID THAT WELL!
IT'S THE FIRST TIME HE'S SAID IT IN VERSE, TOO!
IN OTHER WORDS: START SPENDING LESS!!
I'VE MADE A LIST OF ITEMS WE'LL NEED TO CUT OUT IMMEDIATELY... FIRST ITEM!...
I HEARD HIM LOUD AND CLEAR! FIRST ITEM: BUDDY!... REDUCE THE AMOUNT OF SUGAR CUBES, MARROW BONES, BISCUITS AND BLAHBLAHBLI AND BLAHBLAHBLAH!...

You've Gotta Have a Nose for It!

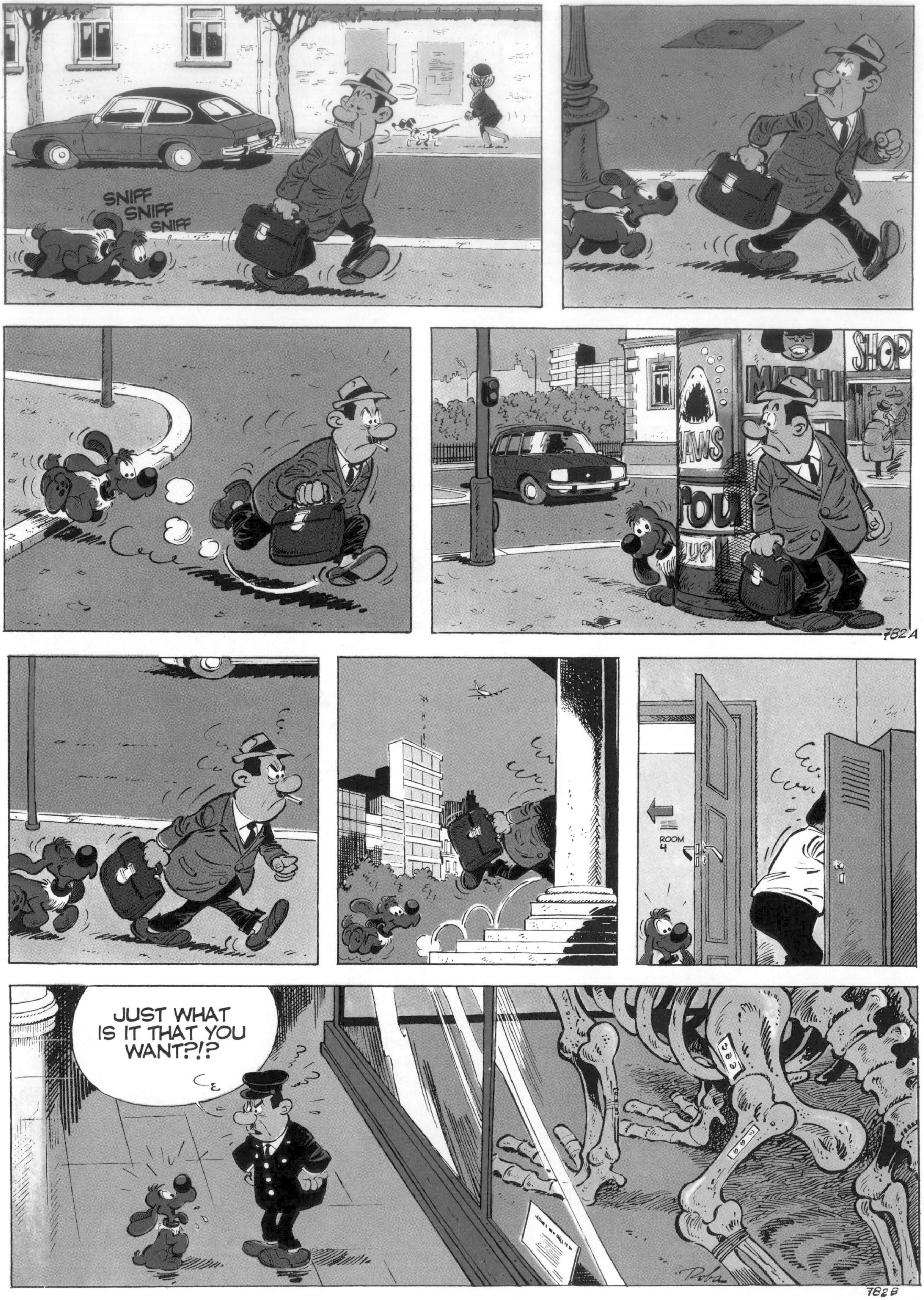
SNIFF
SNIFF
SNIFF
JAWS
SHOP
ROOM 4
JUST WHAT IS IT THAT YOU WANT?!?
782 A
782 B

March on, Scouts!

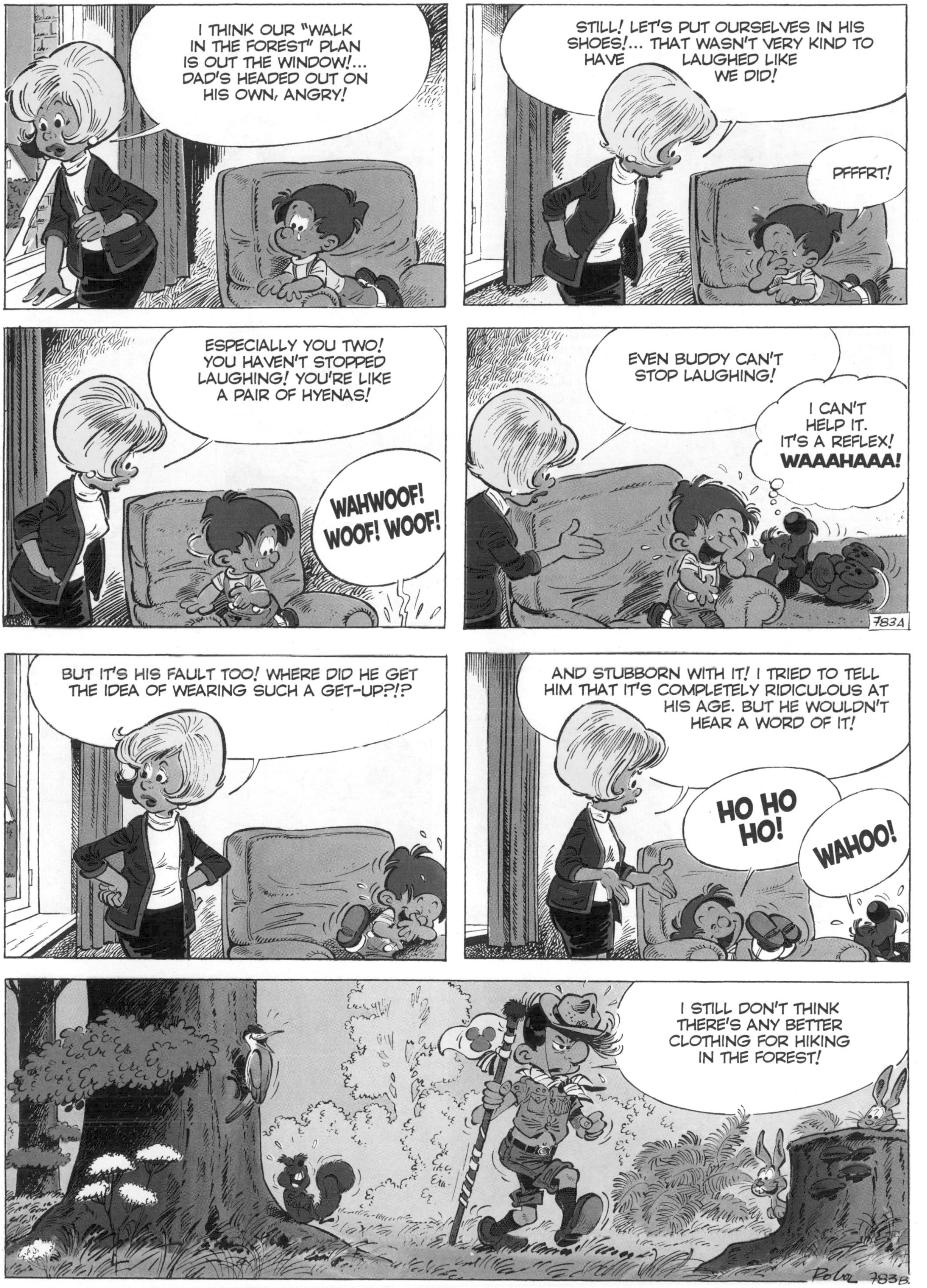

I THINK OUR "WALK IN THE FOREST" PLAN IS OUT THE WINDOW!... DAD'S HEADED OUT ON HIS OWN, ANGRY!
STILL! LET'S PUT OURSELVES IN HIS SHOES!... THAT WASN'T VERY KIND TO HAVE LAUGHED LIKE WE DID!
PFFFRT!
ESPECIALLY YOU TWO! YOU HAVEN'T STOPPED LAUGHING! YOU'RE LIKE A PAIR OF HYENAS!
WAHWOOF! WOOF! WOOF!
EVEN BUDDY CAN'T STOP LAUGHING!
I CAN'T HELP IT. IT'S A REFLEX! WAAAHAAA!
783A
BUT IT'S HIS FAULT TOO! WHERE DID HE GET THE IDEA OF WEARING SUCH A GET-UP?!?
AND STUBBORN WITH IT! I TRIED TO TELL HIM THAT IT'S COMPLETELY RIDICULOUS AT HIS AGE. BUT HE WOULDN'T HEAR A WORD OF IT!
HO HO HO!
WAHOO!
I STILL DON'T THINK THERE'S ANY BETTER CLOTHING FOR HIKING IN THE FOREST!
783B.

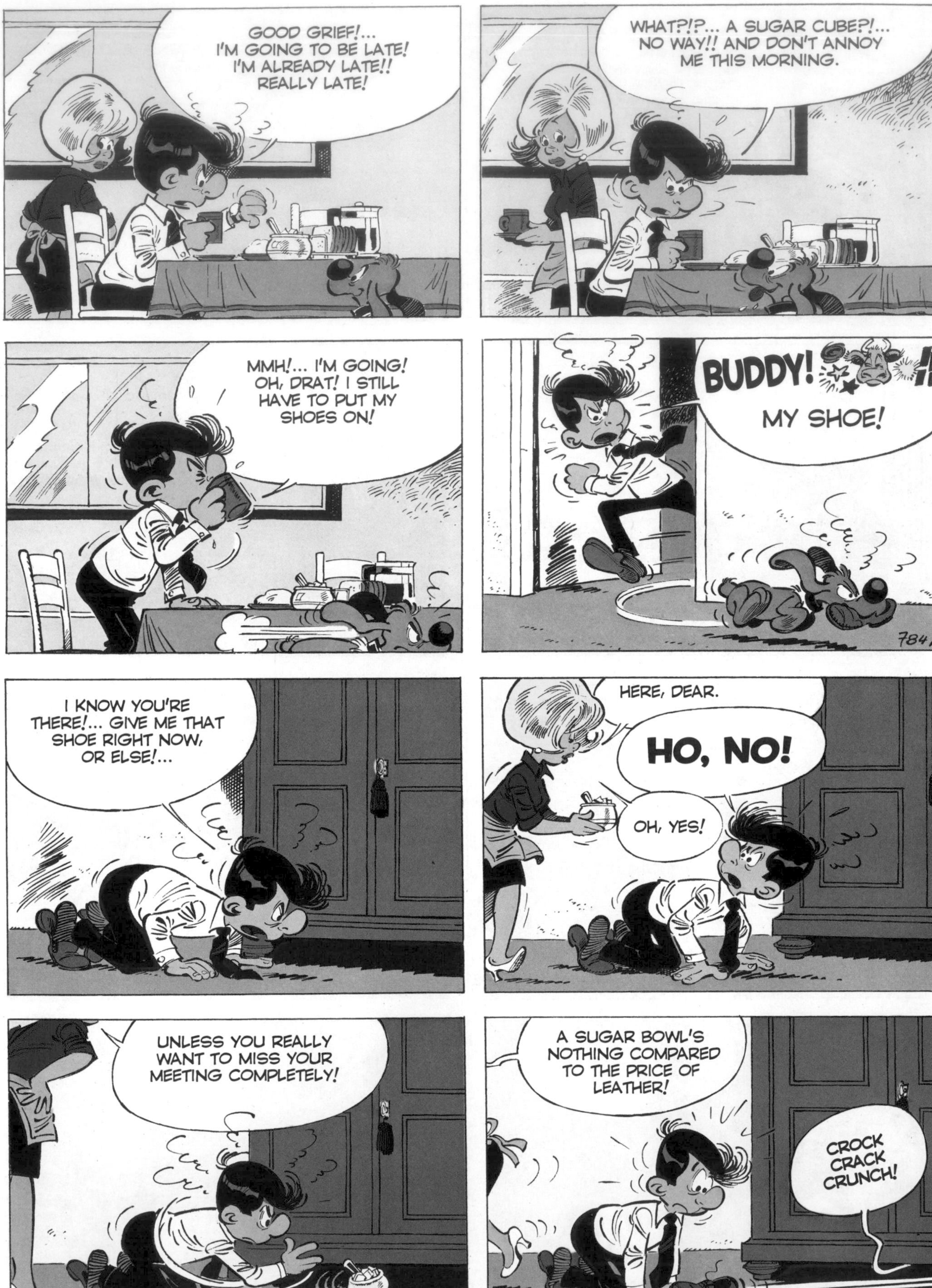
GOOD GRIEF!... I'M GOING TO BE LATE! I'M ALREADY LATE!! REALLY LATE!
WHAT?!?... A SUGAR CUBE?!... NO WAY!! AND DON'T ANNOY ME THIS MORNING.
MMH!... I'M GOING! OH, DRAT! I STILL HAVE TO PUT MY SHOES ON!
BUDDY!
MY SHOE!
784 A
I KNOW YOU'RE THERE!... GIVE ME THAT SHOE RIGHT NOW, OR ELSE!...
HERE, DEAR.
HO, NO!
OH, YES!
UNLESS YOU REALLY WANT TO MISS YOUR MEETING COMPLETELY!
A SUGAR BOWL'S NOTHING COMPARED TO THE PRICE OF LEATHER!
CROCK CRACK CRUNCH!
Roba 784 B

Watering Can('t)

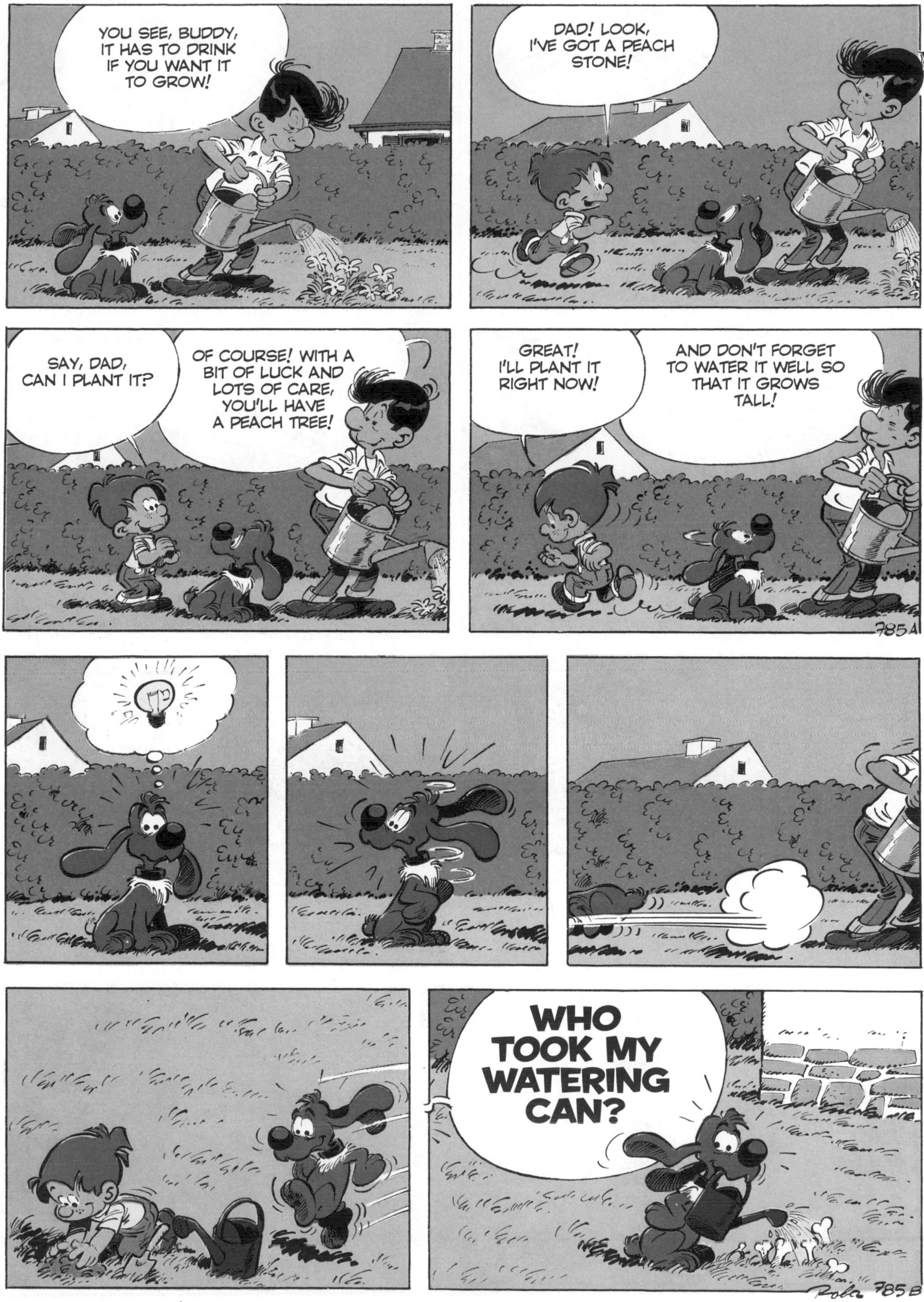
YOU SEE, BUDDY, IT HAS TO DRINK IF YOU WANT IT TO GROW!
DAD! LOOK, I'VE GOT A PEACH STONE!
SAY, DAD, CAN I PLANT IT?
OF COURSE! WITH A BIT OF LUCK AND LOTS OF CARE, YOU'LL HAVE A PEACH TREE!
GREAT! I'LL PLANT IT RIGHT NOW!
AND DON'T FORGET TO WATER IT WELL SO THAT IT GROWS TALL!
785A
WHO TOOK MY WATERING CAN?
Roba 785B

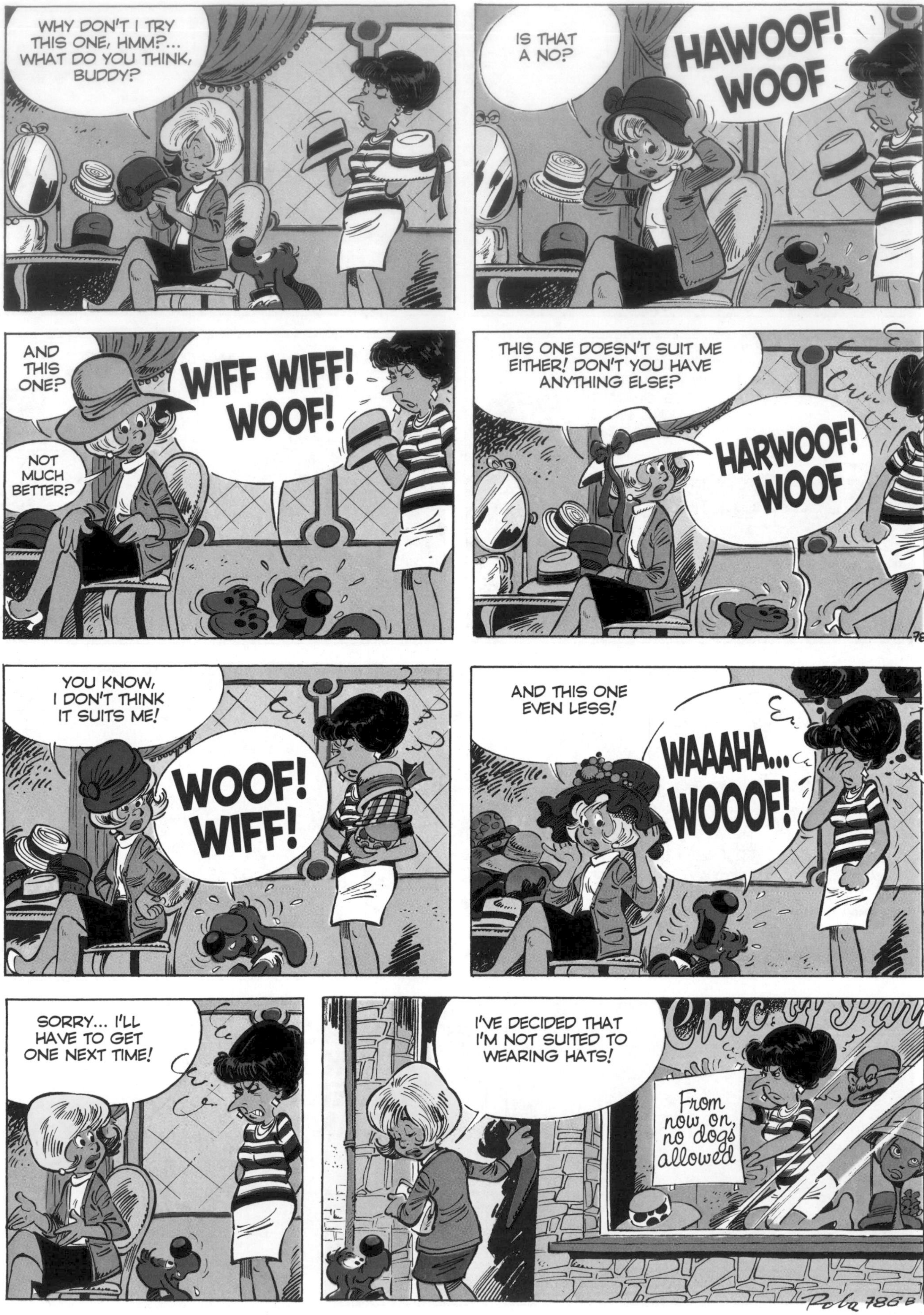
WHY DON'T I TRY THIS ONE, HMM?... WHAT DO YOU THINK, BUDDY?
IS THAT A NO?
HAWOOF! WOOF
AND THIS ONE?
WIFF WIFF! WOOF!
NOT MUCH BETTER?
THIS ONE DOESN'T SUIT ME EITHER! DON'T YOU HAVE ANYTHING ELSE?
HARWOOF! WOOF
786A
YOU KNOW, I DON'T THINK IT SUITS ME!
WOOF! WIFF!
AND THIS ONE EVEN LESS!
WAAAHA... WOOOF!
SORRY... I'LL HAVE TO GET ONE NEXT TIME!
I'VE DECIDED THAT I'M NOT SUITED TO WEARING HATS!
From now on, no dogs allowed
Roba 786B

Greenfingers

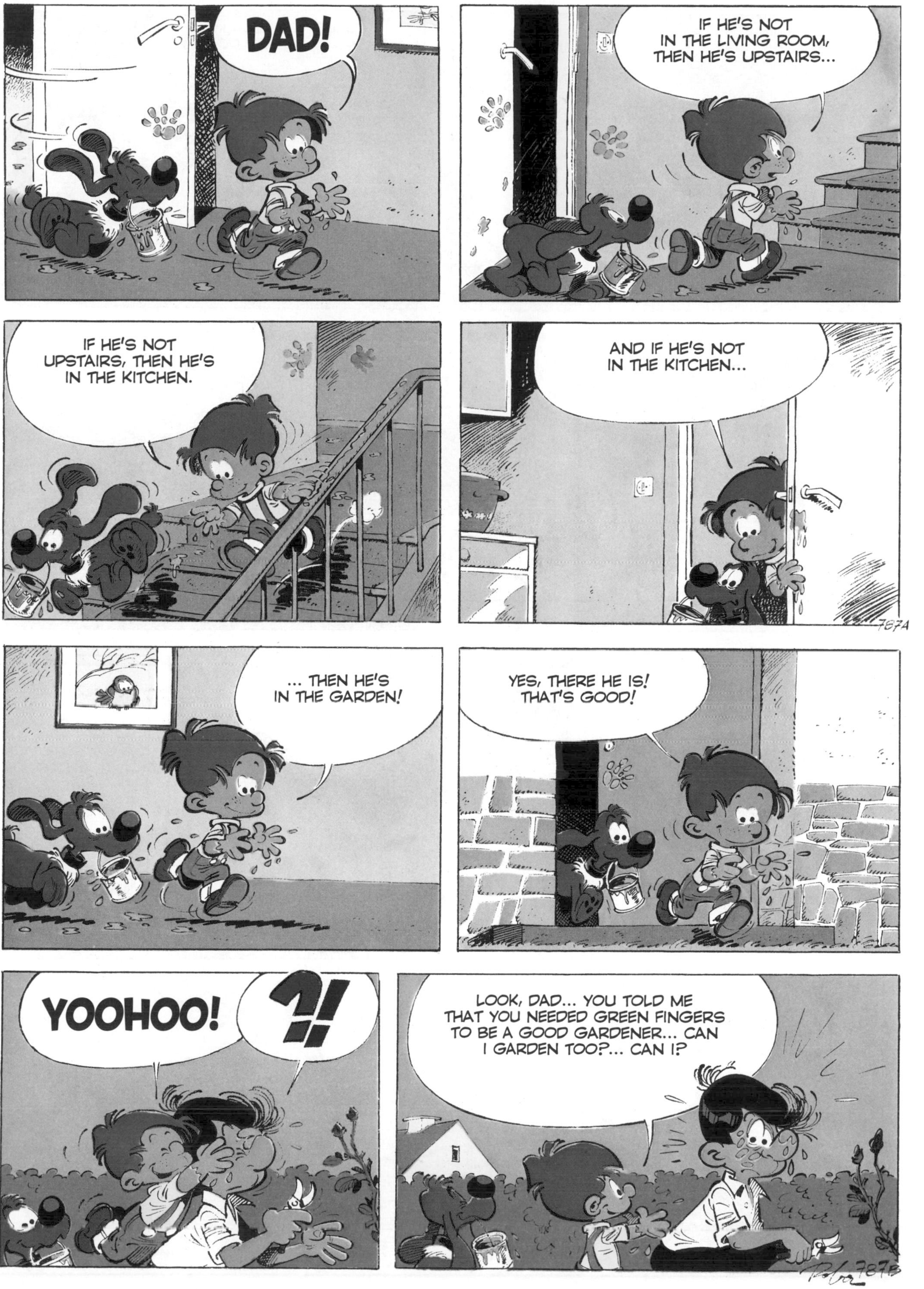

DAD!
IF HE'S NOT IN THE LIVING ROOM, THEN HE'S UPSTAIRS...
IF HE'S NOT UPSTAIRS, THEN HE'S IN THE KITCHEN.
AND IF HE'S NOT IN THE KITCHEN...
... THEN HE'S IN THE GARDEN!
YES, THERE HE IS! THAT'S GOOD!
YOOHOO!
?!
LOOK, DAD... YOU TOLD ME THAT YOU NEEDED GREEN FINGERS TO BE A GOOD GARDENER... CAN I GARDEN TOO?... CAN I?

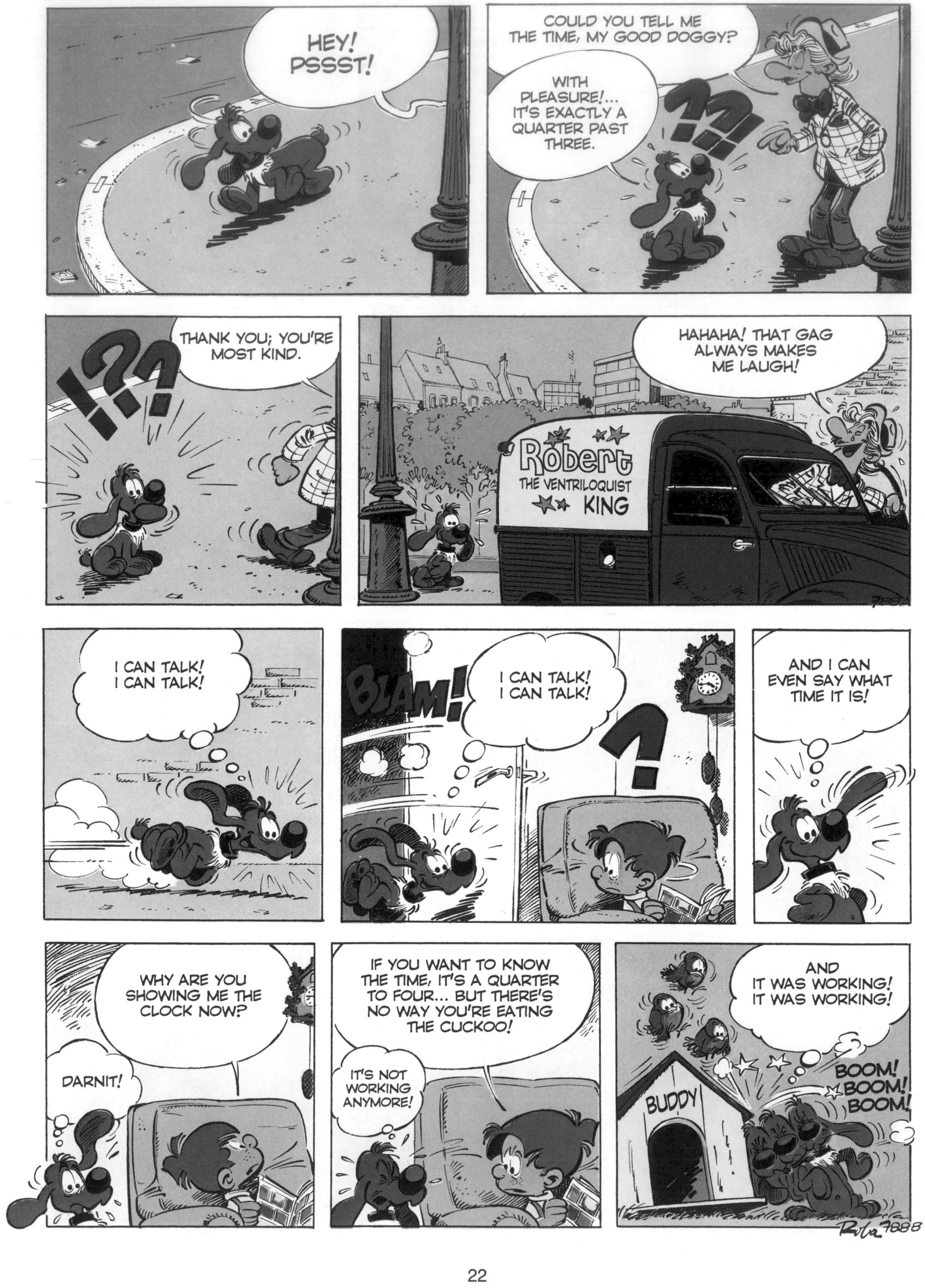
HEY! PSSST!
COULD YOU TELL ME THE TIME, MY GOOD DOGGY?
WITH PLEASURE!... IT'S EXACTLY A QUARTER PAST THREE.
THANK YOU; YOU'RE MOST KIND.
HAHAHA! THAT GAG ALWAYS MAKES ME LAUGH!
Robert THE VENTRILOQUIST KING
I CAN TALK! I CAN TALK!
BLAM!
I CAN TALK! I CAN TALK!
AND I CAN EVEN SAY WHAT TIME IT IS!
WHY ARE YOU SHOWING ME THE CLOCK NOW?
DARNIT!
IF YOU WANT TO KNOW THE TIME, IT'S A QUARTER TO FOUR... BUT THERE'S NO WAY YOU'RE EATING THE CUCKOO!
IT'S NOT WORKING ANYMORE!
AND IT WAS WORKING! IT WAS WORKING!
BUDDY
BOOM! BOOM! BOOM!

Inboxed

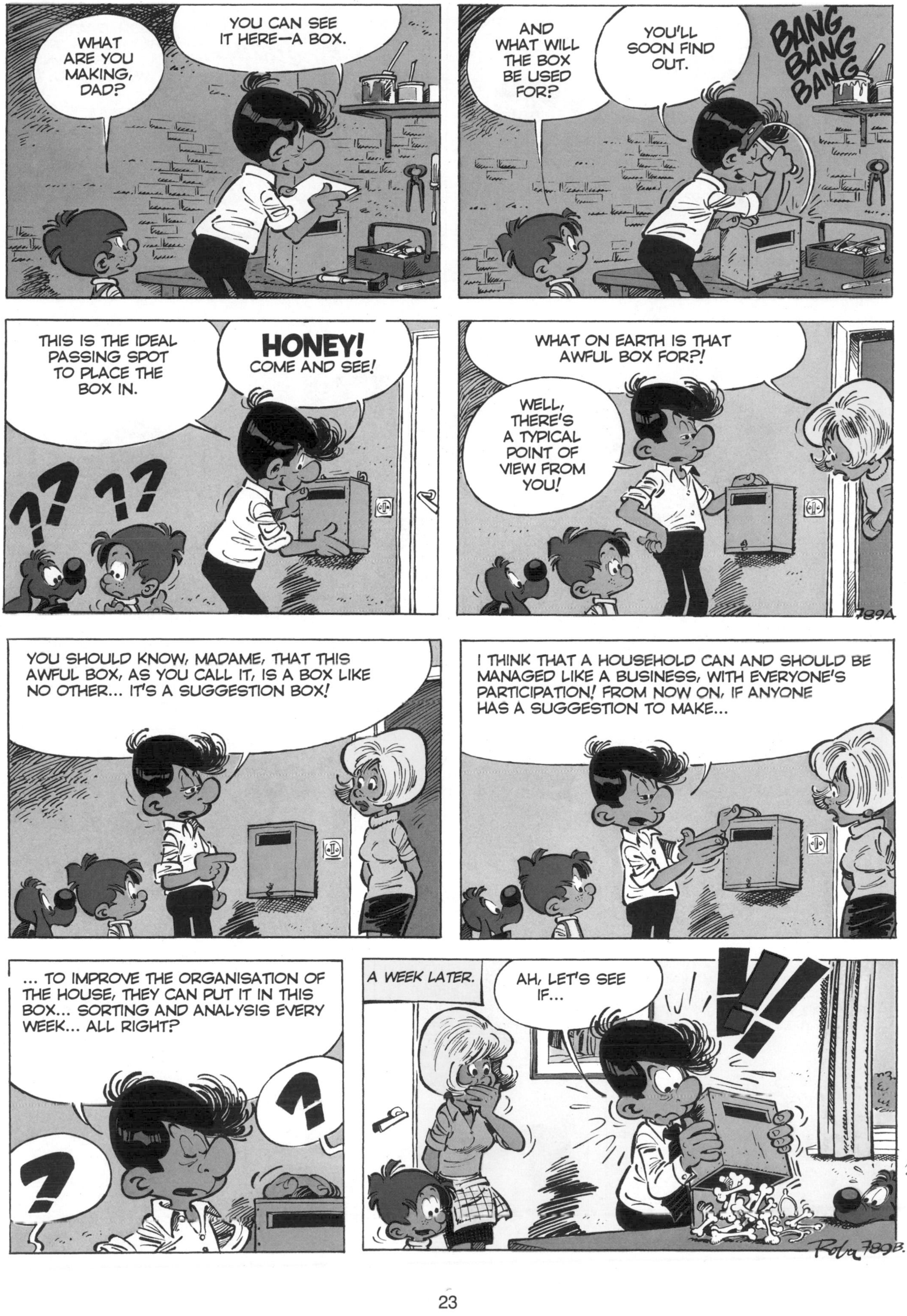
WHAT ARE YOU MAKING, DAD?
YOU CAN SEE IT HERE—A BOX.
AND WHAT WILL THE BOX BE USED FOR?
YOU'LL SOON FIND OUT.
BANG BANG BANG
THIS IS THE IDEAL PASSING SPOT TO PLACE THE BOX IN.
HONEY! COME AND SEE!
??
??
WHAT ON EARTH IS THAT AWFUL BOX FOR?!
WELL, THERE'S A TYPICAL POINT OF VIEW FROM YOU!
789A
YOU SHOULD KNOW, MADAME, THAT THIS AWFUL BOX, AS YOU CALL IT, IS A BOX LIKE NO OTHER... IT'S A SUGGESTION BOX!
I THINK THAT A HOUSEHOLD CAN AND SHOULD BE MANAGED LIKE A BUSINESS, WITH EVERYONE'S PARTICIPATION! FROM NOW ON, IF ANYONE HAS A SUGGESTION TO MAKE...
... TO IMPROVE THE ORGANISATION OF THE HOUSE, THEY CAN PUT IT IN THIS BOX... SORTING AND ANALYSIS EVERY WEEK... ALL RIGHT?
?
?
A WEEK LATER.
AH, LET'S SEE IF...
!!!
Roba 789B.

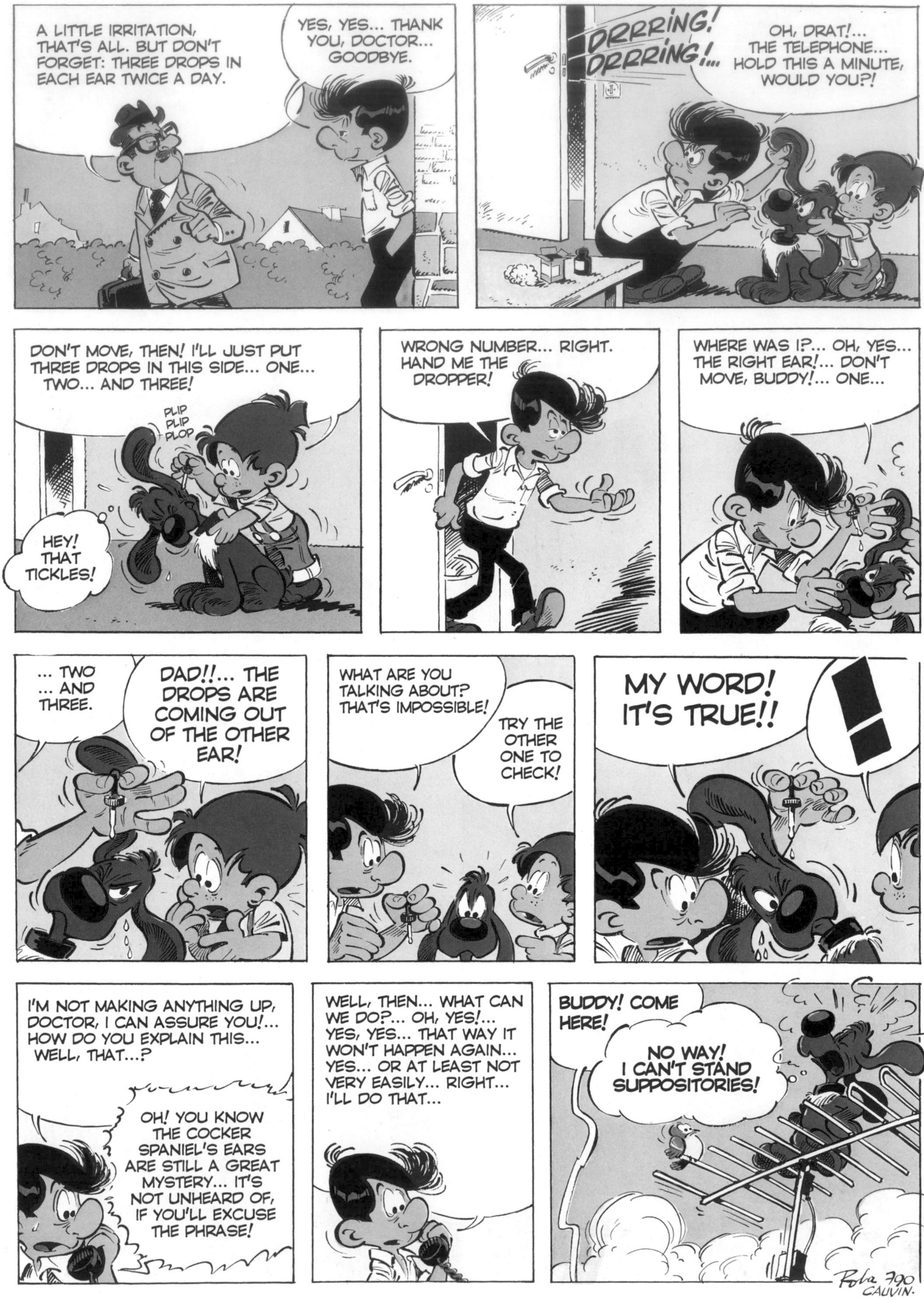
A LITTLE IRRITATION, THAT'S ALL. BUT DON'T FORGET: THREE DROPS IN EACH EAR TWICE A DAY.
YES, YES... THANK YOU, DOCTOR... GOODBYE.
DRRRING! DRRRING!...
OH, DRAT!... THE TELEPHONE... HOLD THIS A MINUTE, WOULD YOU?!
DON'T MOVE, THEN! I'LL JUST PUT THREE DROPS IN THIS SIDE... ONE... TWO... AND THREE!
PLIP PLIP PLOP
HEY! THAT TICKLES!
WRONG NUMBER... RIGHT. HAND ME THE DROPPER!
WHERE WAS I?... OH, YES... THE RIGHT EAR!... DON'T MOVE, BUDDY!... ONE...
... TWO ... AND THREE.
DAD!!... THE DROPS ARE COMING OUT OF THE OTHER EAR!
WHAT ARE YOU TALKING ABOUT? THAT'S IMPOSSIBLE!
TRY THE OTHER ONE TO CHECK!
MY WORD! IT'S TRUE!!
I'M NOT MAKING ANYTHING UP, DOCTOR, I CAN ASSURE YOU!... HOW DO YOU EXPLAIN THIS... WELL, THAT...?
OH! YOU KNOW THE COCKER SPANIEL'S EARS ARE STILL A GREAT MYSTERY... IT'S NOT UNHEARD OF, IF YOU'LL EXCUSE THE PHRASE!
WELL, THEN... WHAT CAN WE DO?... OH, YES!... YES, YES... THAT WAY IT WON'T HAPPEN AGAIN... YES... OR AT LEAST NOT VERY EASILY... RIGHT... I'LL DO THAT...
BUDDY! COME HERE!
NO WAY! I CAN'T STAND SUPPOSITORIES!
Roba 790 CAUVIN.

Come and Go

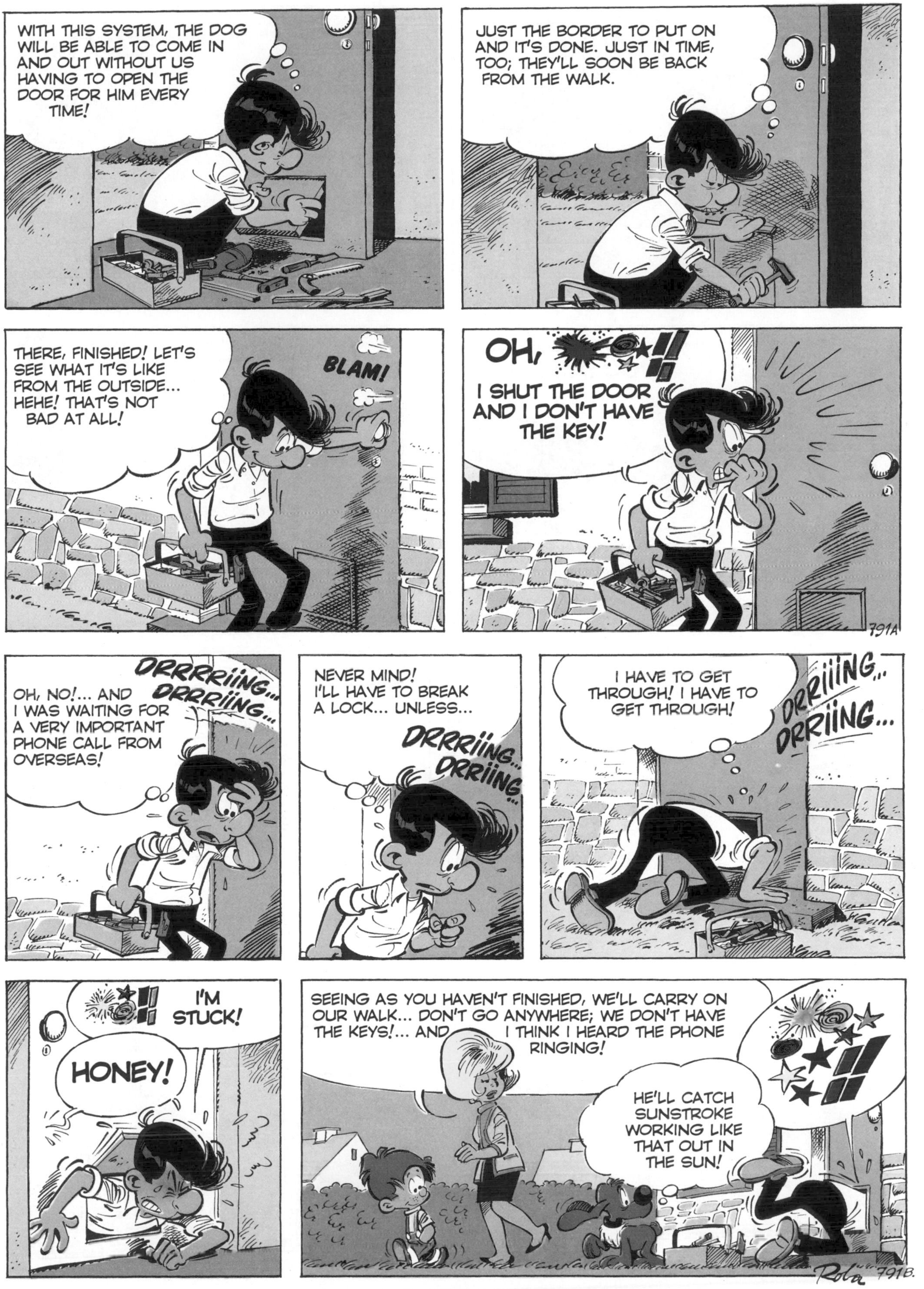
WITH THIS SYSTEM, THE DOG WILL BE ABLE TO COME IN AND OUT WITHOUT US HAVING TO OPEN THE DOOR FOR HIM EVERY TIME!
JUST THE BORDER TO PUT ON AND IT'S DONE. JUST IN TIME, TOO; THEY'LL SOON BE BACK FROM THE WALK.
THERE, FINISHED! LET'S SEE WHAT IT'S LIKE FROM THE OUTSIDE... HEHE! THAT'S NOT BAD AT ALL!
BLAM!
OH, !!
I SHUT THE DOOR AND I DON'T HAVE THE KEY!
791A
OH, NO!... AND I WAS WAITING FOR A VERY IMPORTANT PHONE CALL FROM OVERSEAS!
ORRRRIING... DRRRIING...
NEVER MIND! I'LL HAVE TO BREAK A LOCK... UNLESS...
DRRRIING... DRRIING...
I HAVE TO GET THROUGH! I HAVE TO GET THROUGH!
DRRIIING... DRRIING...
I'M STUCK!
HONEY!
SEEING AS YOU HAVEN'T FINISHED, WE'LL CARRY ON OUR WALK... DON'T GO ANYWHERE; WE DON'T HAVE THE KEYS!... AND I THINK I HEARD THE PHONE RINGING!
HE'LL CATCH SUNSTROKE WORKING LIKE THAT OUT IN THE SUN!
Roba 791B.

Falling in Line

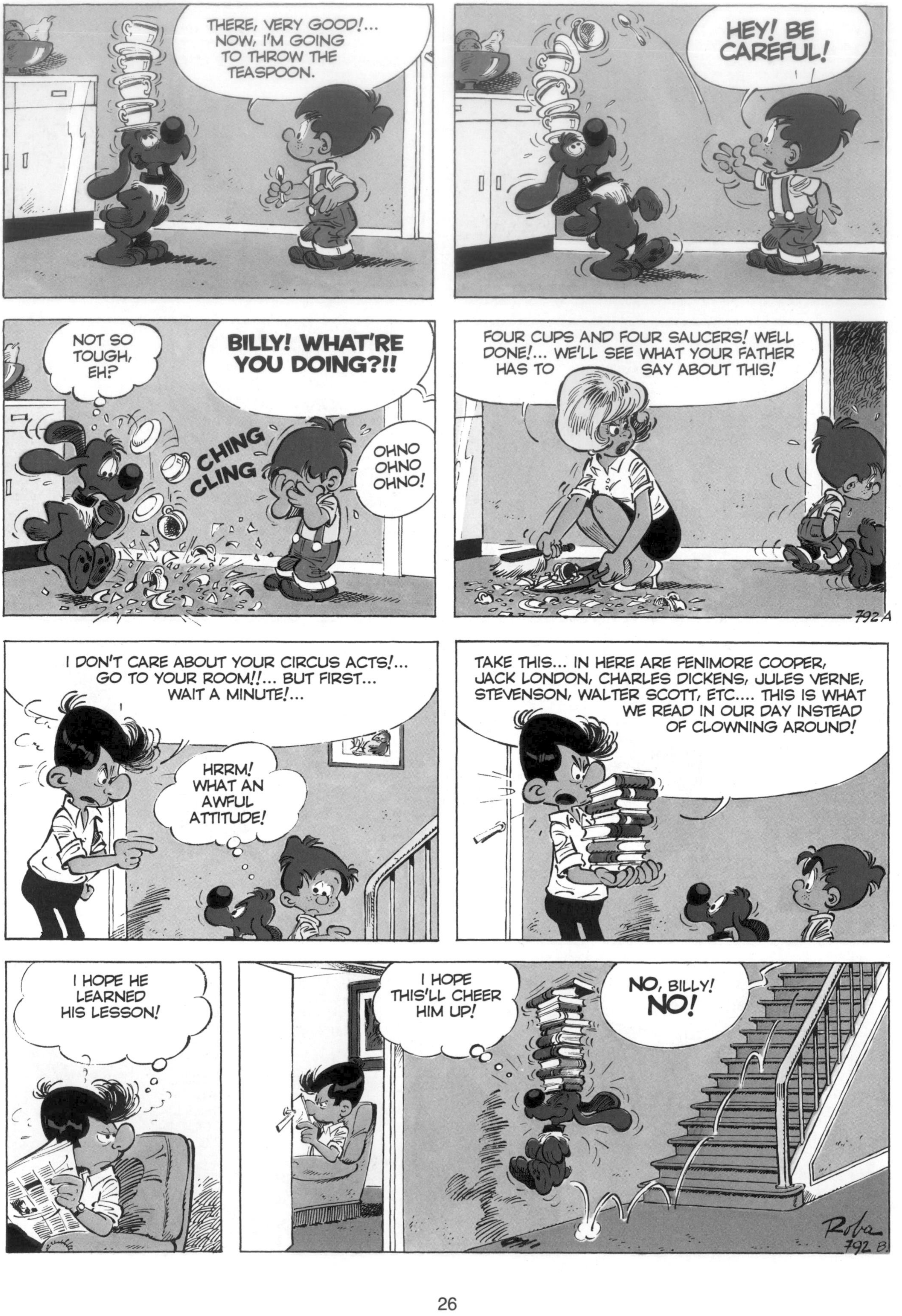

THERE, VERY GOOD!... NOW, I'M GOING TO THROW THE TEASPOON.
HEY! BE CAREFUL!
NOT SO TOUGH, EH?
BILLY! WHAT'RE YOU DOING?!!
CHING CLING
OHNO OHNO OHNO!
FOUR CUPS AND FOUR SAUCERS! WELL DONE!... WE'LL SEE WHAT YOUR FATHER HAS TO SAY ABOUT THIS!
792 A
I DON'T CARE ABOUT YOUR CIRCUS ACTS!... GO TO YOUR ROOM!!... BUT FIRST... WAIT A MINUTE!...
HRRM! WHAT AN AWFUL ATTITUDE!
TAKE THIS... IN HERE ARE FENIMORE COOPER, JACK LONDON, CHARLES DICKENS, JULES VERNE, STEVENSON, WALTER SCOTT, ETC.... THIS IS WHAT WE READ IN OUR DAY INSTEAD OF CLOWNING AROUND!
I HOPE HE LEARNED HIS LESSON!
I HOPE THIS'LL CHEER HIM UP!
NO, BILLY! NO!
Roba
792 B

The Protest

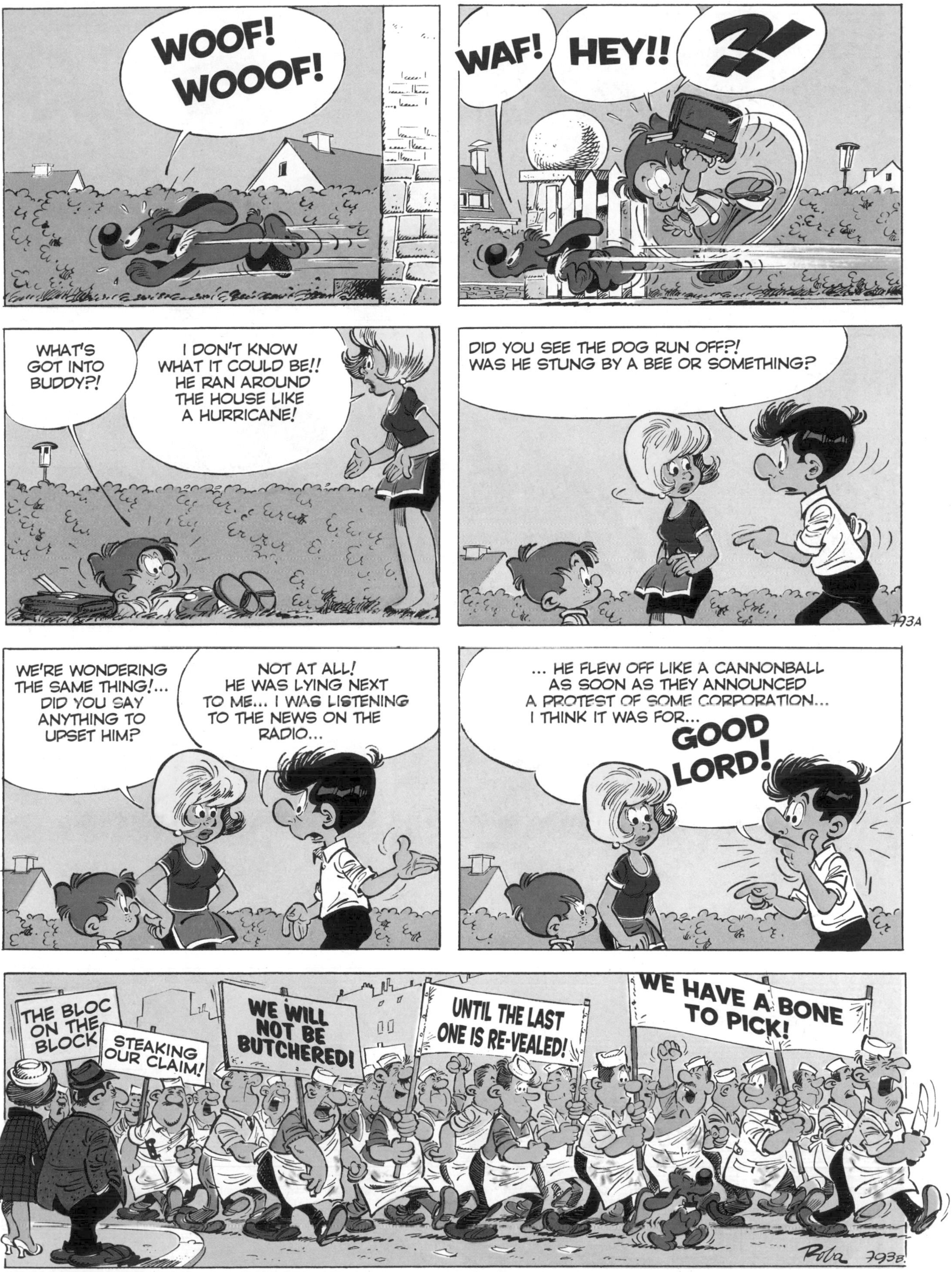
WOOF! WOOOF!
WAF!
HEY!!
?!
WHAT'S GOT INTO BUDDY?!
I DON'T KNOW WHAT IT COULD BE!! HE RAN AROUND THE HOUSE LIKE A HURRICANE!
DID YOU SEE THE DOG RUN OFF?! WAS HE STUNG BY A BEE OR SOMETHING?
793A
WE'RE WONDERING THE SAME THING!... DID YOU SAY ANYTHING TO UPSET HIM?
NOT AT ALL! HE WAS LYING NEXT TO ME... I WAS LISTENING TO THE NEWS ON THE RADIO...
... HE FLEW OFF LIKE A CANNONBALL AS SOON AS THEY ANNOUNCED A PROTEST OF SOME CORPORATION... I THINK IT WAS FOR...
GOOD LORD!
THE BLOC ON THE BLOCK
STEAKING OUR CLAIM!
WE WILL NOT BE BUTCHERED!
UNTIL THE LAST ONE IS RE-VEALED!
WE HAVE A BONE TO PICK!
Roba
793B.

Dog Tags

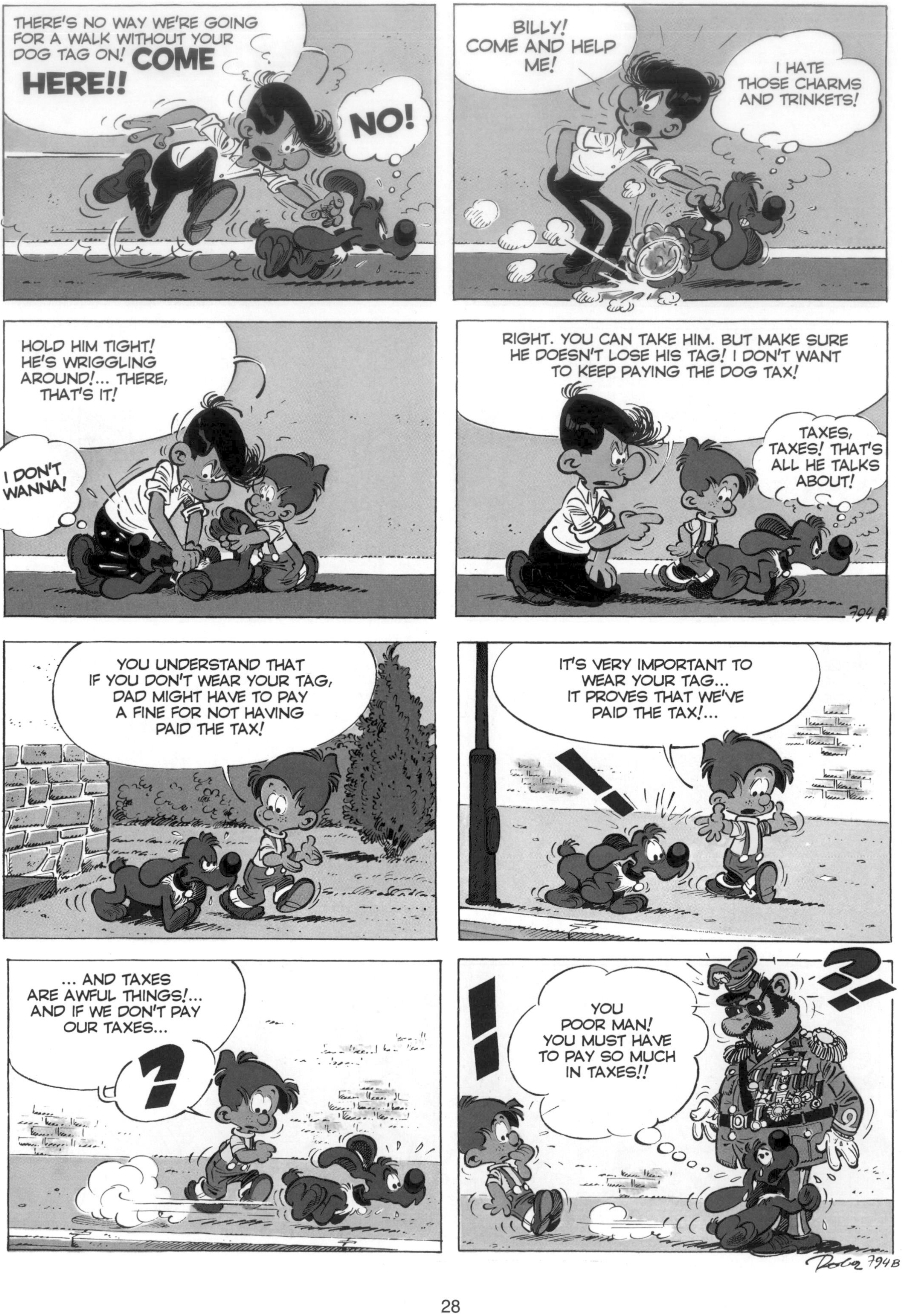

THERE'S NO WAY WE'RE GOING FOR A WALK WITHOUT YOUR DOG TAG ON! COME HERE!!
NO!
BILLY! COME AND HELP ME!
I HATE THOSE CHARMS AND TRINKETS!
HOLD HIM TIGHT! HE'S WRIGGLING AROUND!... THERE, THAT'S IT!
I DON'T WANNA!
RIGHT. YOU CAN TAKE HIM. BUT MAKE SURE HE DOESN'T LOSE HIS TAG! I DON'T WANT TO KEEP PAYING THE DOG TAX!
TAXES, TAXES! THAT'S ALL HE TALKS ABOUT!
YOU UNDERSTAND THAT IF YOU DON'T WEAR YOUR TAG, DAD MIGHT HAVE TO PAY A FINE FOR NOT HAVING PAID THE TAX!
IT'S VERY IMPORTANT TO WEAR YOUR TAG... IT PROVES THAT WE'VE PAID THE TAX!...
!
... AND TAXES ARE AWFUL THINGS!... AND IF WE DON'T PAY OUR TAXES...
?
!
YOU POOR MAN! YOU MUST HAVE TO PAY SO MUCH IN TAXES!!
?!

We're Going In

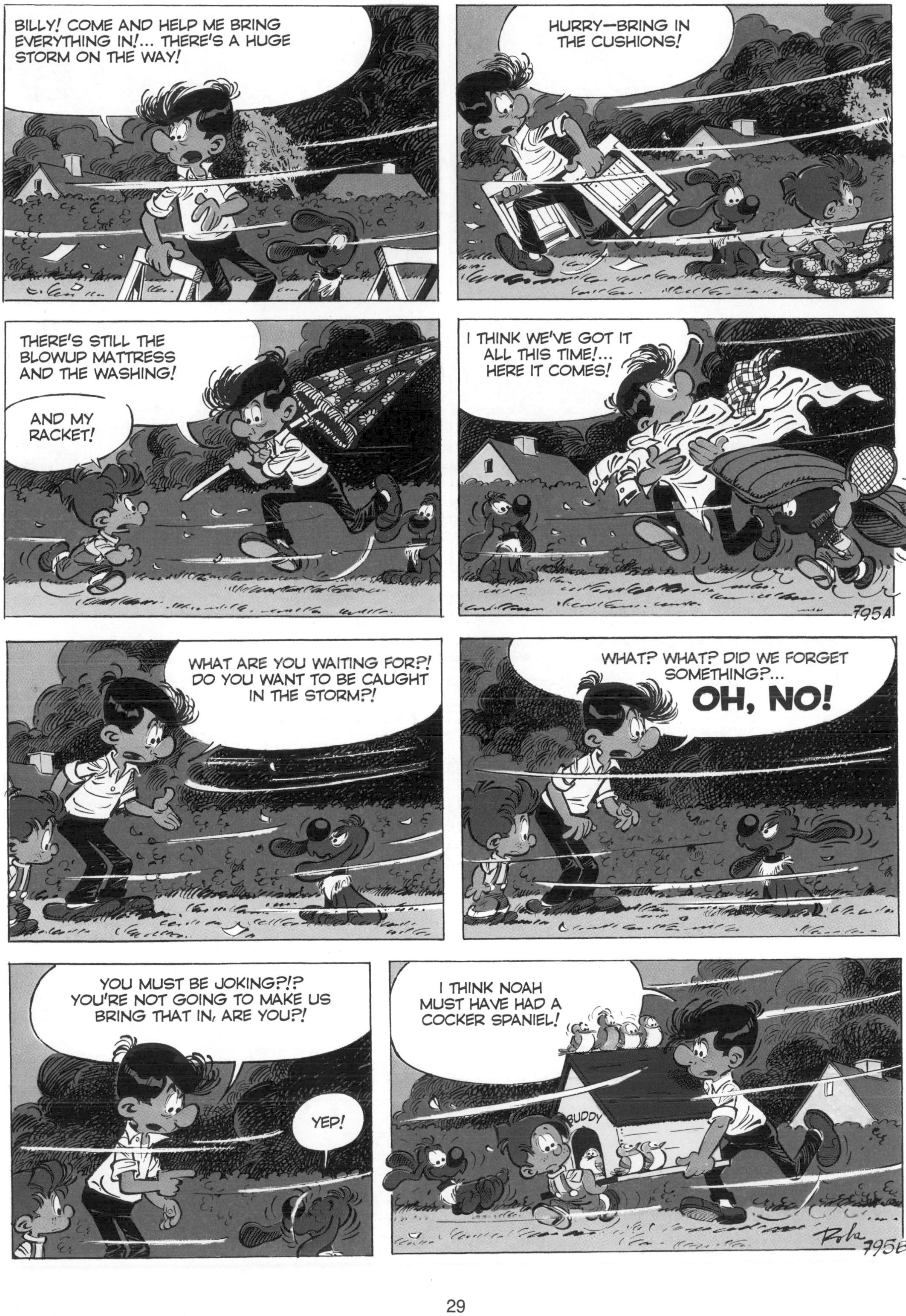
BILLY! COME AND HELP ME BRING EVERYTHING IN!... THERE'S A HUGE STORM ON THE WAY!
HURRY—BRING IN THE CUSHIONS!
THERE'S STILL THE BLOWUP MATTRESS AND THE WASHING!
AND MY RACKET!
I THINK WE'VE GOT IT ALL THIS TIME!... HERE IT COMES!
795A
WHAT ARE YOU WAITING FOR?! DO YOU WANT TO BE CAUGHT IN THE STORM?!
WHAT? WHAT? DID WE FORGET SOMETHING?...
OH, NO!
YOU MUST BE JOKING?!? YOU'RE NOT GOING TO MAKE US BRING THAT IN, ARE YOU?!
YEP!
I THINK NOAH MUST HAVE HAD A COCKER SPANIEL!
BUDDY
795B

Starry Night

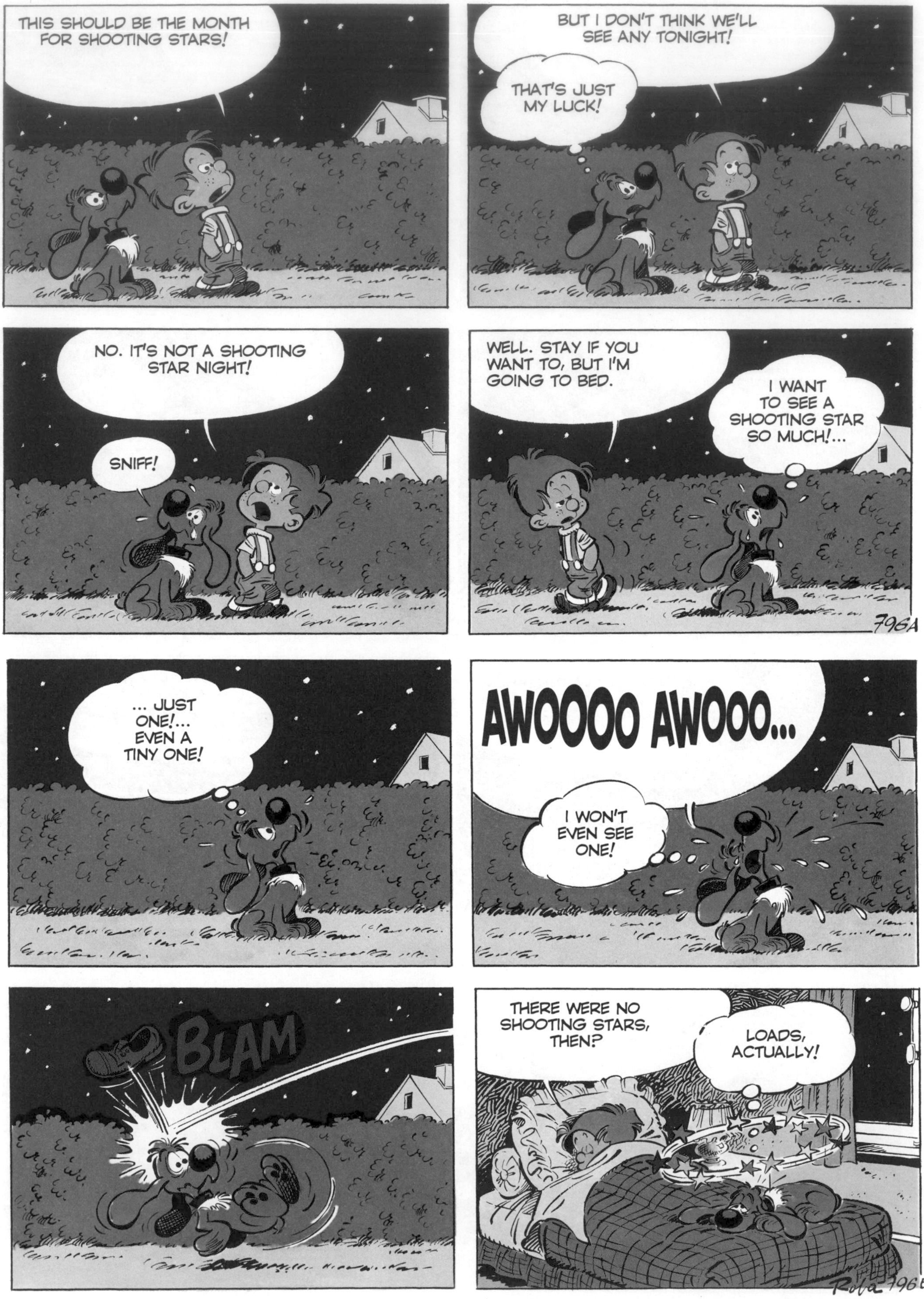
THIS SHOULD BE THE MONTH FOR SHOOTING STARS!
BUT I DON'T THINK WE'LL SEE ANY TONIGHT!
THAT'S JUST MY LUCK!
NO. IT'S NOT A SHOOTING STAR NIGHT!
SNIFF!
WELL. STAY IF YOU WANT TO, BUT I'M GOING TO BED.
I WANT TO SEE A SHOOTING STAR SO MUCH!...
796A
... JUST ONE!... EVEN A TINY ONE!
AWOOOO AWOOO...
I WON'T EVEN SEE ONE!
BLAM
THERE WERE NO SHOOTING STARS, THEN?
LOADS, ACTUALLY!
Roba 796B

Odds On

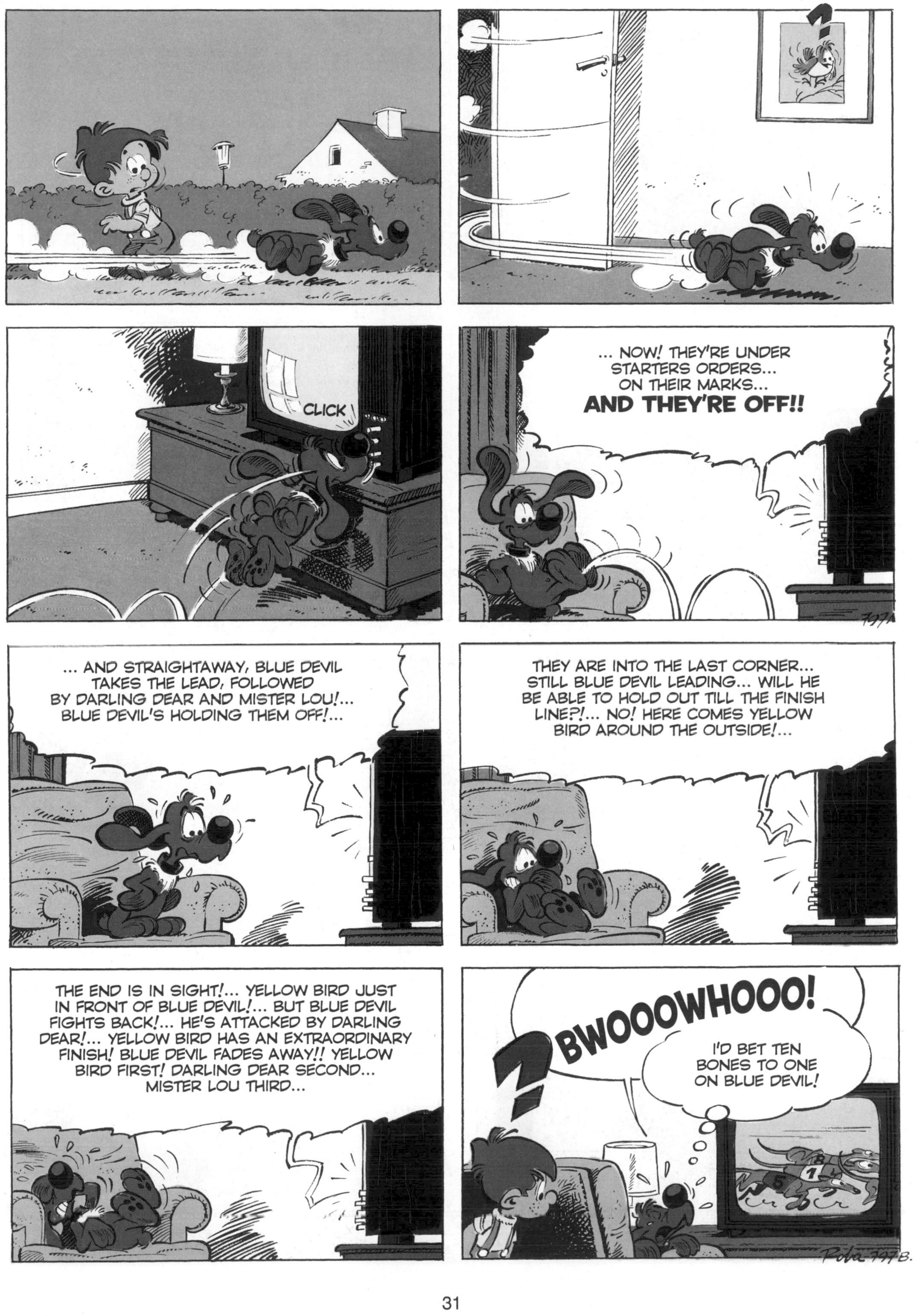

CLICK
... NOW! THEY'RE UNDER STARTERS ORDERS... ON THEIR MARKS... AND THEY'RE OFF!!
... AND STRAIGHTAWAY, BLUE DEVIL TAKES THE LEAD, FOLLOWED BY DARLING DEAR AND MISTER LOU!... BLUE DEVIL'S HOLDING THEM OFF!...
THEY ARE INTO THE LAST CORNER... STILL BLUE DEVIL LEADING... WILL HE BE ABLE TO HOLD OUT TILL THE FINISH LINE?!... NO! HERE COMES YELLOW BIRD AROUND THE OUTSIDE!...
THE END IS IN SIGHT!... YELLOW BIRD JUST IN FRONT OF BLUE DEVIL!... BUT BLUE DEVIL FIGHTS BACK!... HE'S ATTACKED BY DARLING DEAR!... YELLOW BIRD HAS AN EXTRAORDINARY FINISH! BLUE DEVIL FADES AWAY!! YELLOW BIRD FIRST! DARLING DEAR SECOND... MISTER LOU THIRD...
BWOOOWHOOO!
I'D BET TEN BONES TO ONE ON BLUE DEVIL!

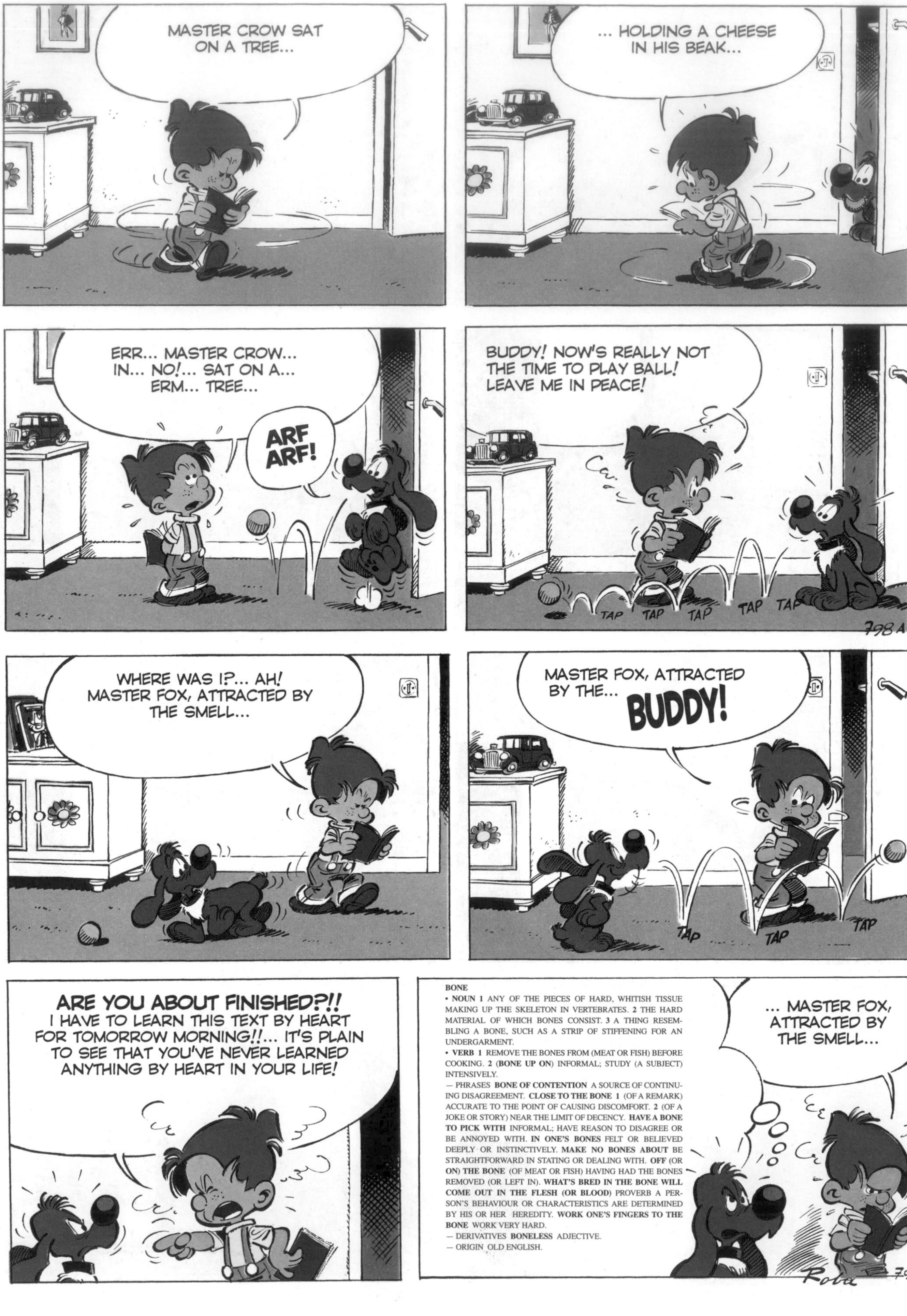
MASTER CROW SAT ON A TREE...
... HOLDING A CHEESE IN HIS BEAK...
ERR... MASTER CROW... IN... NO!... SAT ON A... ERM... TREE...
ARF ARF!
BUDDY! NOW'S REALLY NOT THE TIME TO PLAY BALL! LEAVE ME IN PEACE!
TAP TAP TAP TAP TAP
798 A
WHERE WAS I?... AH! MASTER FOX, ATTRACTED BY THE SMELL...
MASTER FOX, ATTRACTED BY THE...
BUDDY!
TAP TAP TAP
ARE YOU ABOUT FINISHED?!! I HAVE TO LEARN THIS TEXT BY HEART FOR TOMORROW MORNING!!... IT'S PLAIN TO SEE THAT YOU'VE NEVER LEARNED ANYTHING BY HEART IN YOUR LIFE!
BONE
• NOUN 1 ANY OF THE PIECES OF HARD, WHITISH TISSUE MAKING UP THE SKELETON IN VERTEBRATES. 2 THE HARD MATERIAL OF WHICH BONES CONSIST. 3 A THING RESEMBLING A BONE, SUCH AS A STRIP OF STIFFENING FOR AN UNDERGARMENT.
• VERB 1 REMOVE THE BONES FROM (MEAT OR FISH) BEFORE COOKING. 2 (BONE UP ON) INFORMAL; STUDY (A SUBJECT) INTENSIVELY.
— PHRASES BONE OF CONTENTION A SOURCE OF CONTINUING DISAGREEMENT. CLOSE TO THE BONE 1 (OF A REMARK) ACCURATE TO THE POINT OF CAUSING DISCOMFORT. 2 (OF A JOKE OR STORY) NEAR THE LIMIT OF DECENCY. HAVE A BONE TO PICK WITH INFORMAL; HAVE REASON TO DISAGREE OR BE ANNOYED WITH. IN ONE'S BONES FELT OR BELIEVED DEEPLY OR INSTINCTIVELY. MAKE NO BONES ABOUT BE STRAIGHTFORWARD IN STATING OR DEALING WITH. OFF (OR ON) THE BONE (OF MEAT OR FISH) HAVING HAD THE BONES REMOVED (OR LEFT IN). WHAT'S BRED IN THE BONE WILL COME OUT IN THE FLESH (OR BLOOD) PROVERB A PERSON'S BEHAVIOUR OR CHARACTERISTICS ARE DETERMINED BY HIS OR HER HEREDITY. WORK ONE'S FINGERS TO THE BONE WORK VERY HARD.
— DERIVATIVES BONELESS ADJECTIVE.
— ORIGIN OLD ENGLISH.
... MASTER FOX, ATTRACTED BY THE SMELL...
Roba
798 B

The Ga... Gaga... Gaffe

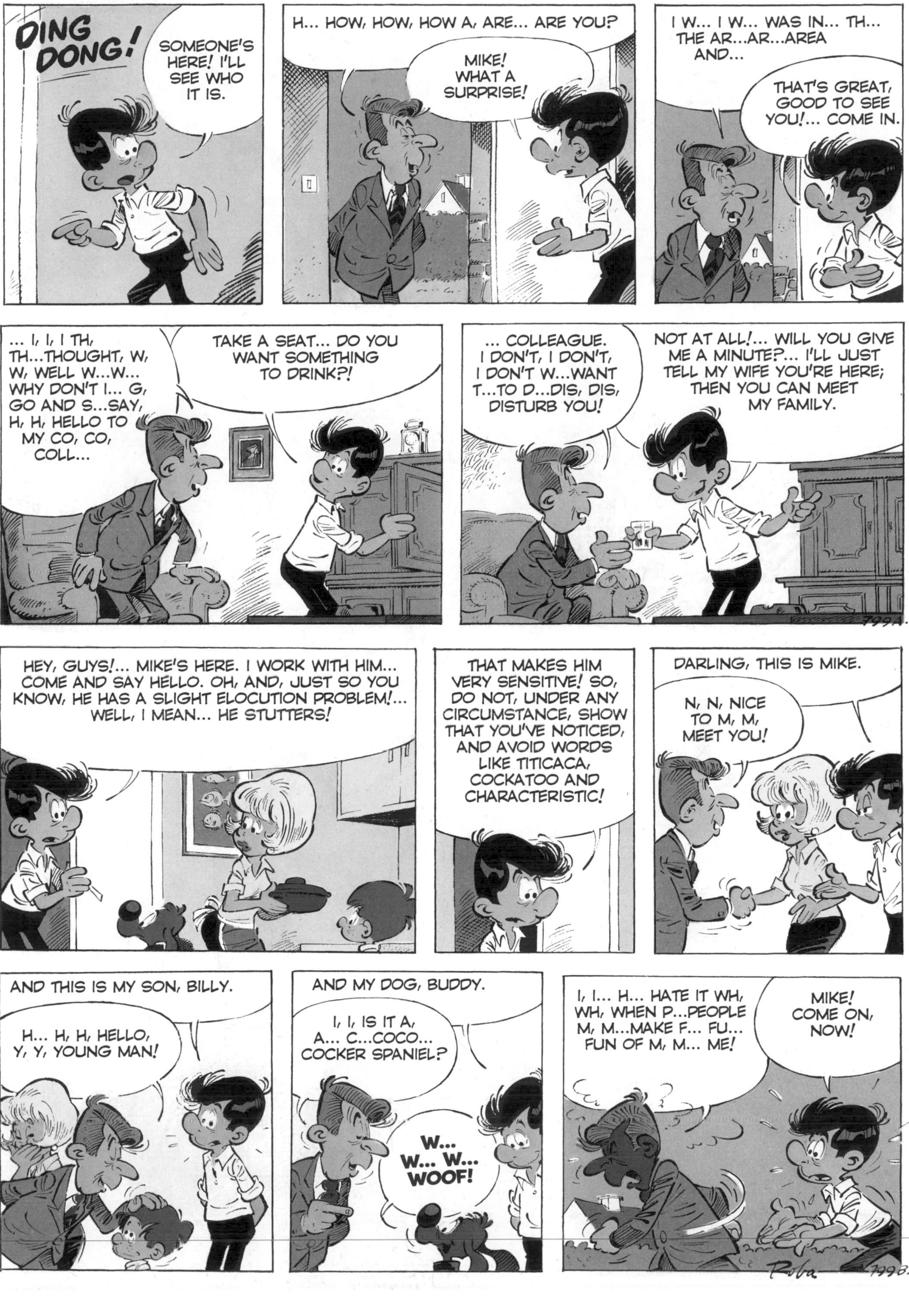
DING DONG!
SOMEONE'S HERE! I'LL SEE WHO IT IS.
H... HOW, HOW, HOW A, ARE... ARE YOU?
MIKE! WHAT A SURPRISE!
I W... I W... WAS IN... TH... THE AR...AR...AREA AND...
THAT'S GREAT, GOOD TO SEE YOU!... COME IN.
... I, I, I TH, TH...THOUGHT, W, W, WELL W...W... WHY DON'T I... G, GO AND S...SAY, H, H, HELLO TO MY CO, CO, COLL...
TAKE A SEAT... DO YOU WANT SOMETHING TO DRINK?!
... COLLEAGUE. I DON'T, I DON'T, I DON'T W...WANT T...TO D...DIS, DIS, DISTURB YOU!
NOT AT ALL!... WILL YOU GIVE ME A MINUTE?... I'LL JUST TELL MY WIFE YOU'RE HERE; THEN YOU CAN MEET MY FAMILY.
HEY, GUYS!... MIKE'S HERE. I WORK WITH HIM... COME AND SAY HELLO. OH, AND, JUST SO YOU KNOW, HE HAS A SLIGHT ELOCUTION PROBLEM!... WELL, I MEAN... HE STUTTERS!
THAT MAKES HIM VERY SENSITIVE! SO, DO NOT, UNDER ANY CIRCUMSTANCE, SHOW THAT YOU'VE NOTICED, AND AVOID WORDS LIKE TITICACA, COCKATOO AND CHARACTERISTIC!
DARLING, THIS IS MIKE.
N, N, NICE TO M, M, MEET YOU!
AND THIS IS MY SON, BILLY.
H... H, H, HELLO, Y, Y, YOUNG MAN!
AND MY DOG, BUDDY.
I, I, IS IT A, A... C...COCO... COCKER SPANIEL?
W... W... W... WOOF!
I, I... H... HATE IT WH, WH, WHEN P...PEOPLE M, M...MAKE F... FU... FUN OF M, M... ME!
MIKE! COME ON, NOW!
Roba

A-A-At Home

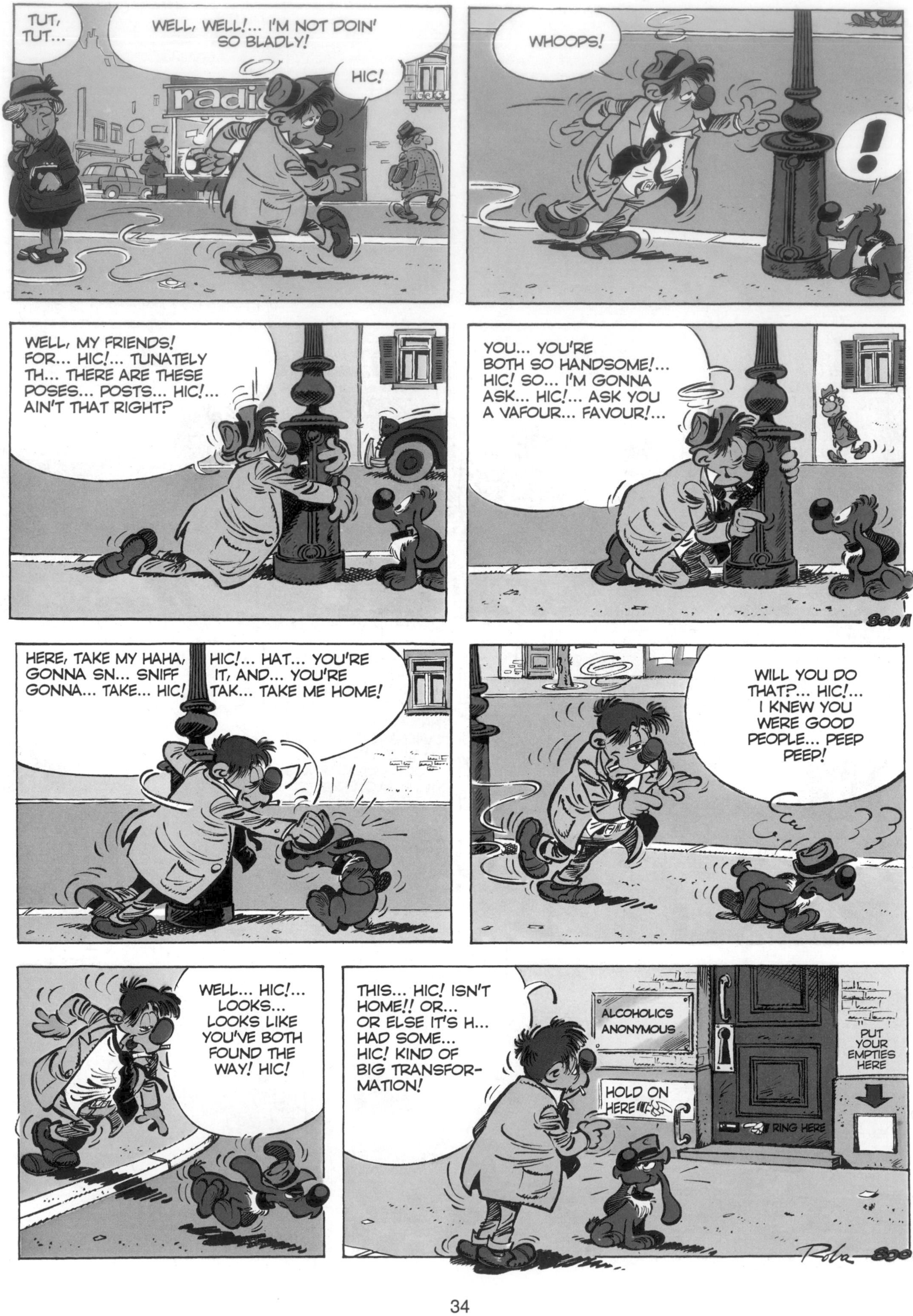

TUT, TUT...
WELL, WELL!... I'M NOT DOIN' SO BLADLY!
HIC!
WHOOPS!
!
WELL, MY FRIENDS! FOR... HIC!... TUNATELY TH... THERE ARE THESE POSES... POSTS... HIC!... AIN'T THAT RIGHT?
YOU... YOU'RE BOTH SO HANDSOME!... HIC! SO... I'M GONNA ASK... HIC!... ASK YOU A VAFOUR... FAVOUR!...
HERE, TAKE MY HAHA, GONNA SN... SNIFF GONNA... TAKE... HIC!
HIC!... HAT... YOU'RE IT, AND... YOU'RE TAK... TAKE ME HOME!
WILL YOU DO THAT?... HIC!... I KNEW YOU WERE GOOD PEOPLE... PEEP PEEP!
WELL... HIC!... LOOKS... LOOKS LIKE YOU'VE BOTH FOUND THE WAY! HIC!
THIS... HIC! ISN'T HOME!! OR... OR ELSE IT'S H... HAD SOME... HIC! KIND OF BIG TRANSFOR-MATION!
ALCOHOLICS ANONYMOUS
HOLD ON HERE
RING HERE
PUT YOUR EMPTIES HERE

Lover's Way

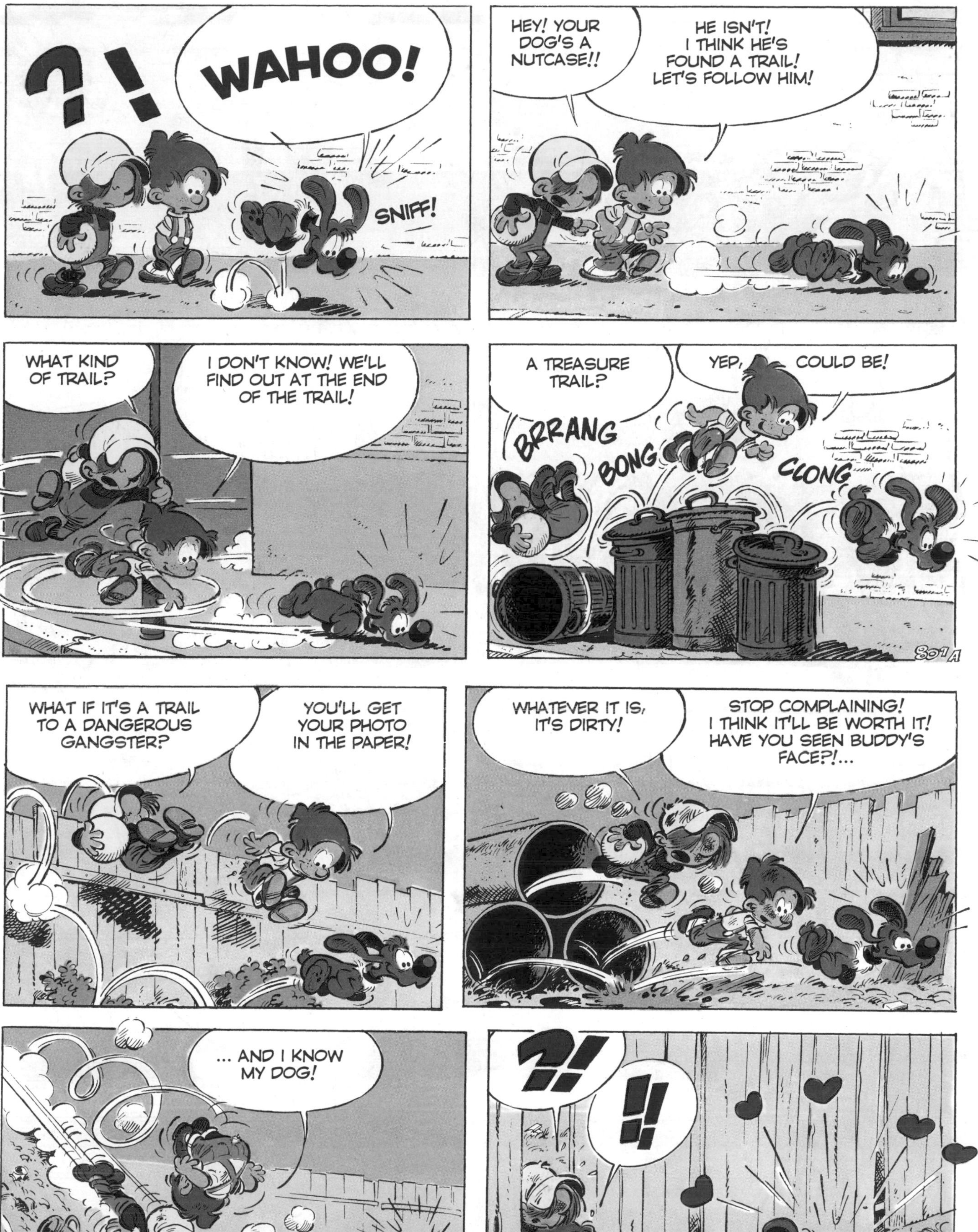

?!
WAHOO!
SNIFF!
HEY! YOUR DOG'S A NUTCASE!!
HE ISN'T! I THINK HE'S FOUND A TRAIL! LET'S FOLLOW HIM!
WHAT KIND OF TRAIL?
I DON'T KNOW! WE'LL FIND OUT AT THE END OF THE TRAIL!
A TREASURE TRAIL?
YEP, COULD BE!
BRRANG
BONG
CLONG
WHAT IF IT'S A TRAIL TO A DANGEROUS GANGSTER?
YOU'LL GET YOUR PHOTO IN THE PAPER!
WHATEVER IT IS, IT'S DIRTY!
STOP COMPLAINING! I THINK IT'LL BE WORTH IT! HAVE YOU SEEN BUDDY'S FACE?!...
... AND I KNOW MY DOG!
?!
!!
Roba

Back from a Weekend Away

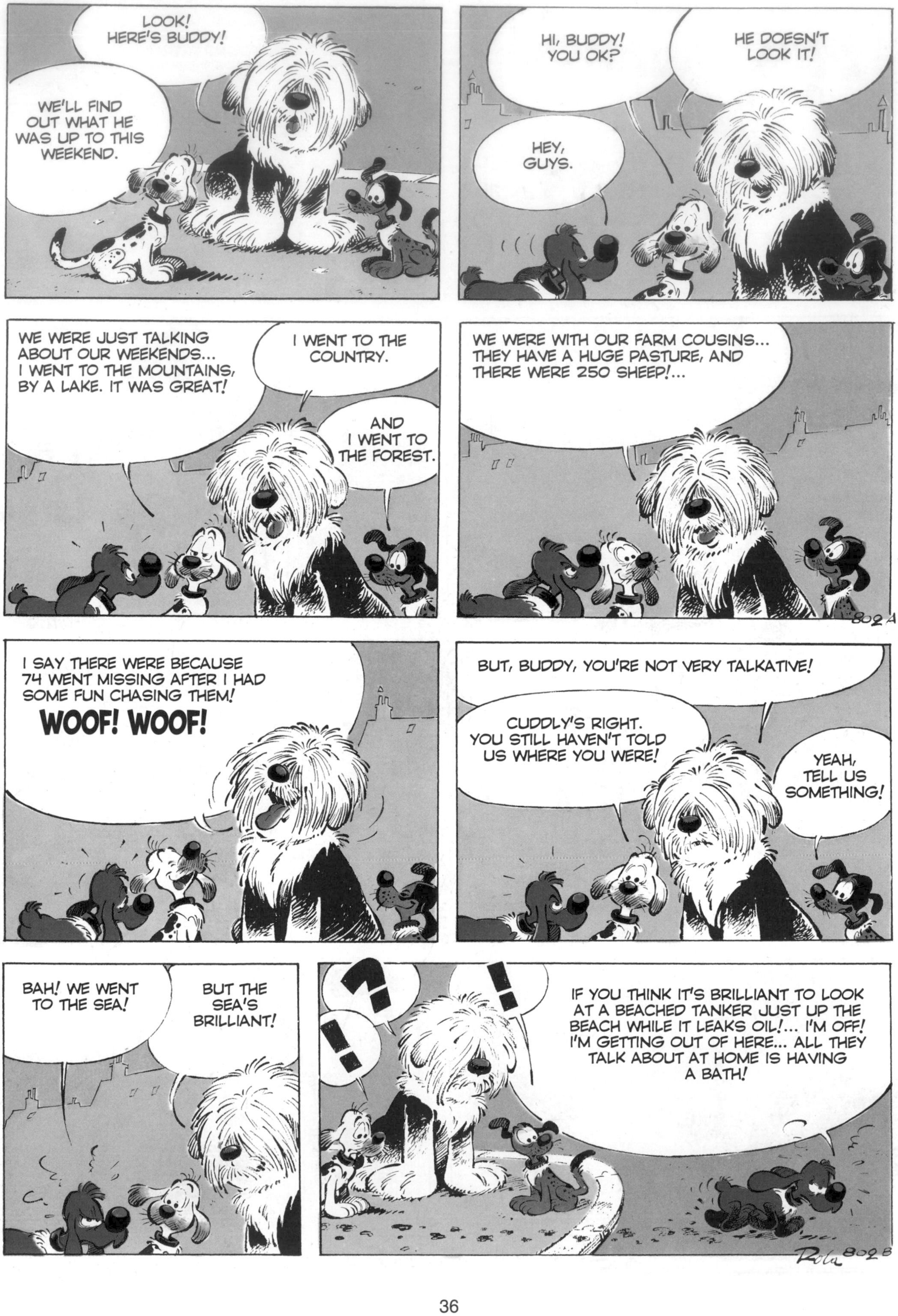

LOOK! HERE'S BUDDY!
WE'LL FIND OUT WHAT HE WAS UP TO THIS WEEKEND.
HI, BUDDY! YOU OK?
HE DOESN'T LOOK IT!
HEY, GUYS.
WE WERE JUST TALKING ABOUT OUR WEEKENDS... I WENT TO THE MOUNTAINS, BY A LAKE. IT WAS GREAT!
I WENT TO THE COUNTRY.
AND I WENT TO THE FOREST.
WE WERE WITH OUR FARM COUSINS... THEY HAVE A HUGE PASTURE, AND THERE WERE 250 SHEEP!...
802 A
I SAY THERE WERE BECAUSE 74 WENT MISSING AFTER I HAD SOME FUN CHASING THEM!
WOOF! WOOF!
BUT, BUDDY, YOU'RE NOT VERY TALKATIVE!
CUDDLY'S RIGHT. YOU STILL HAVEN'T TOLD US WHERE YOU WERE!
YEAH, TELL US SOMETHING!
BAH! WE WENT TO THE SEA!
BUT THE SEA'S BRILLIANT!
?!
!
IF YOU THINK IT'S BRILLIANT TO LOOK AT A BEACHED TANKER JUST UP THE BEACH WHILE IT LEAKS OIL!... I'M OFF! I'M GETTING OUT OF HERE... ALL THEY TALK ABOUT AT HOME IS HAVING A BATH!
Rola 802 B

Pop's Pipe

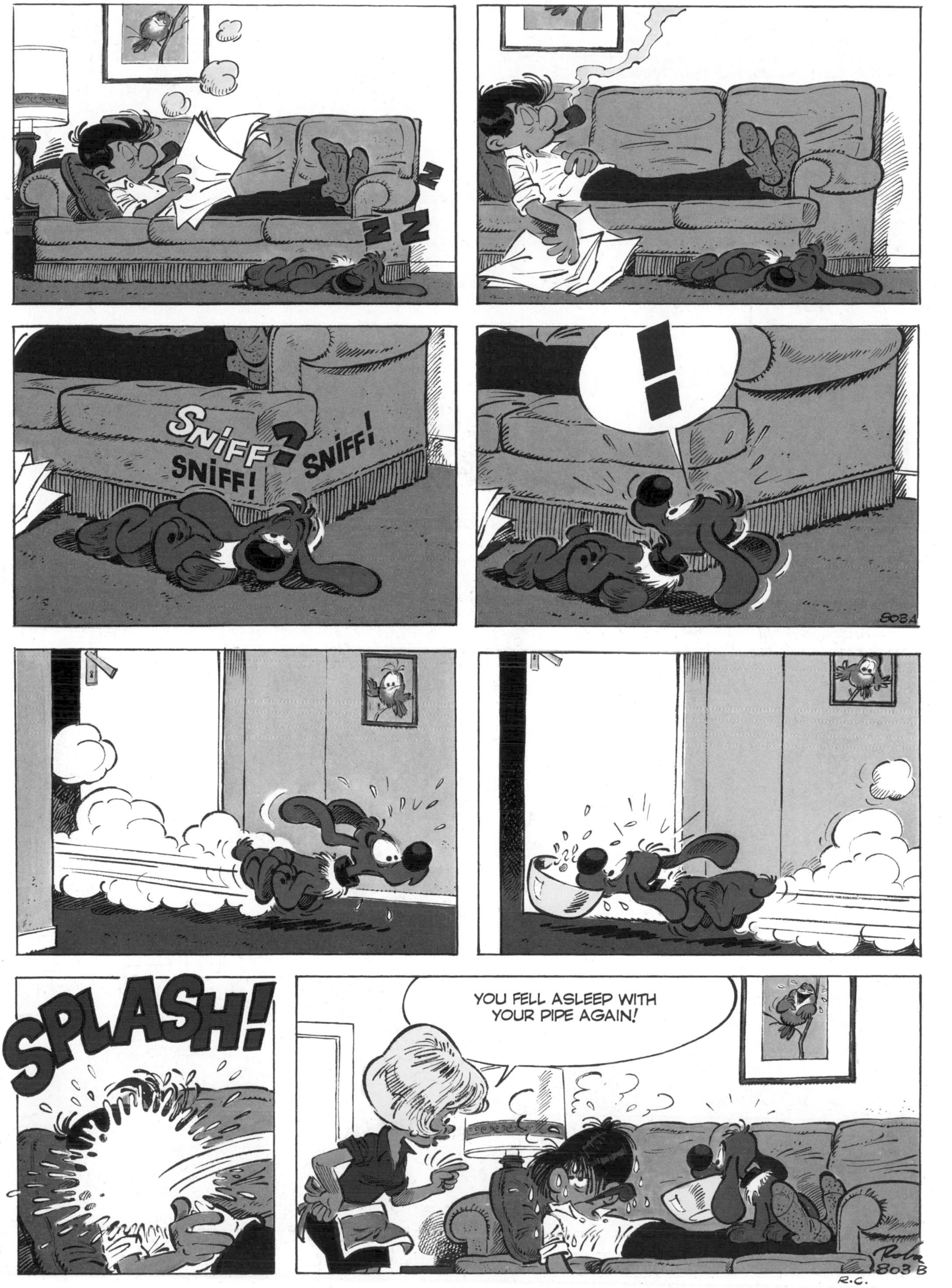
Z
Z Z
SNIFF
SNIFF!
?
SNIFF!
!
SPLASH!
YOU FELL ASLEEP WITH
YOUR PIPE AGAIN!

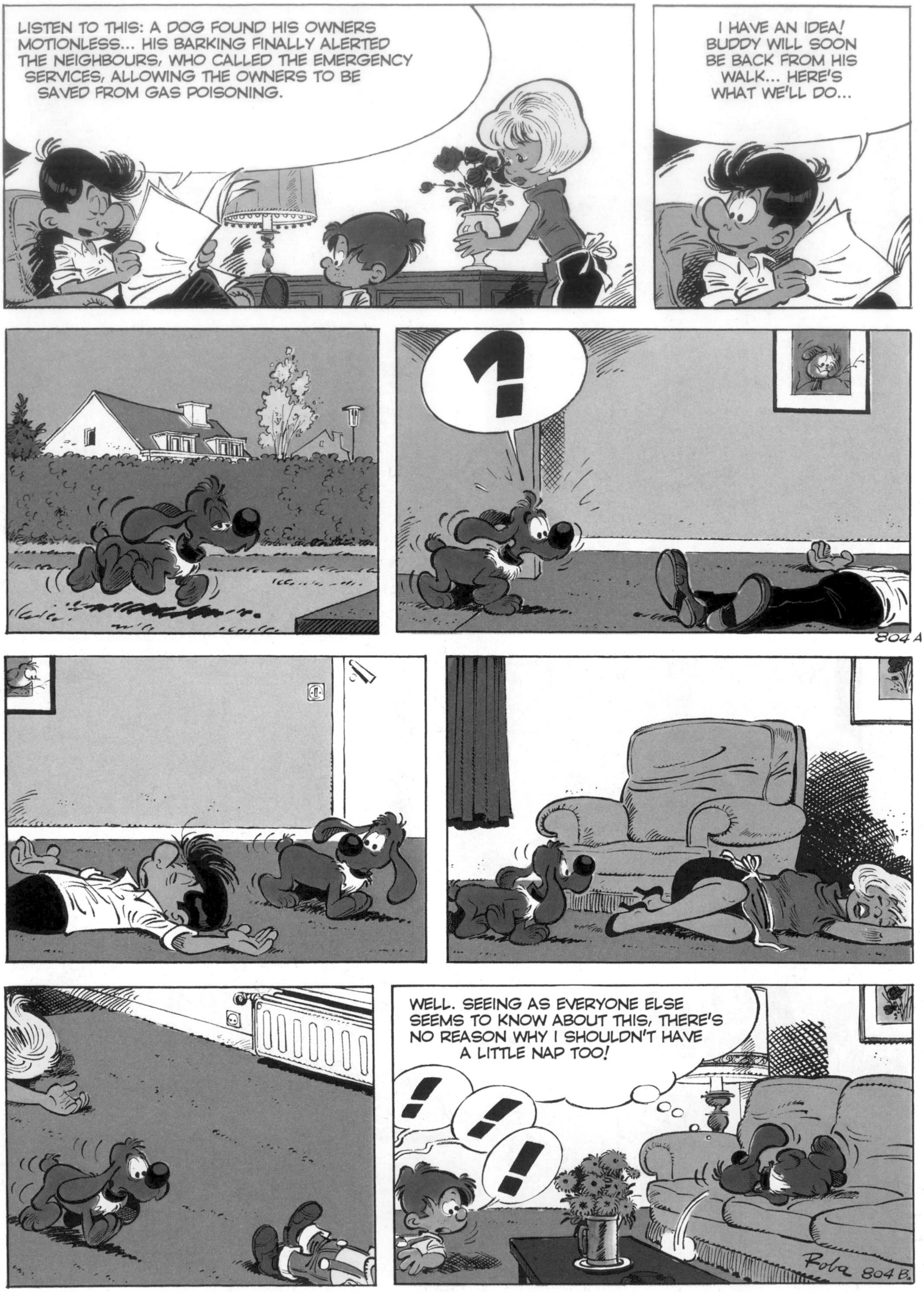
LISTEN TO THIS: A DOG FOUND HIS OWNERS MOTIONLESS... HIS BARKING FINALLY ALERTED THE NEIGHBOURS, WHO CALLED THE EMERGENCY SERVICES, ALLOWING THE OWNERS TO BE SAVED FROM GAS POISONING.
I HAVE AN IDEA! BUDDY WILL SOON BE BACK FROM HIS WALK... HERE'S WHAT WE'LL DO...
804 A
WELL. SEEING AS EVERYONE ELSE SEEMS TO KNOW ABOUT THIS, THERE'S NO REASON WHY I SHOULDN'T HAVE A LITTLE NAP TOO!
Roba 804 B.

Blocked Up

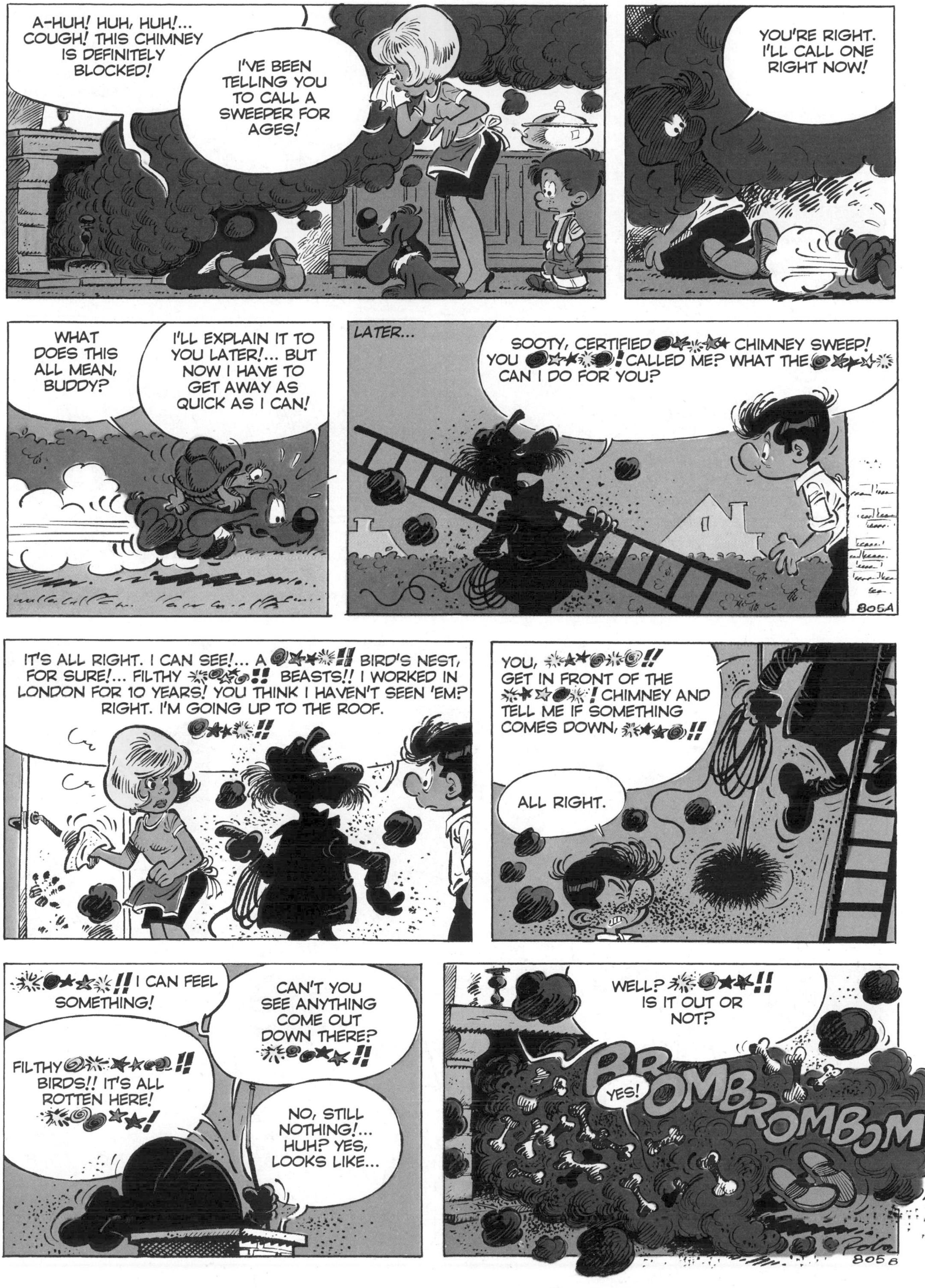

A-HUH! HUH, HUH!... COUGH! THIS CHIMNEY IS DEFINITELY BLOCKED!
I'VE BEEN TELLING YOU TO CALL A SWEEPER FOR AGES!
YOU'RE RIGHT. I'LL CALL ONE RIGHT NOW!
WHAT DOES THIS ALL MEAN, BUDDY?
I'LL EXPLAIN IT TO YOU LATER!... BUT NOW I HAVE TO GET AWAY AS QUICK AS I CAN!
LATER...
SOOTY, CERTIFIED CHIMNEY SWEEP! YOU CALLED ME? WHAT THE CAN I DO FOR YOU?
805A
IT'S ALL RIGHT. I CAN SEE!... A !! BIRD'S NEST, FOR SURE!... FILTHY !! BEASTS!! I WORKED IN LONDON FOR 10 YEARS! YOU THINK I HAVEN'T SEEN 'EM? RIGHT. I'M GOING UP TO THE ROOF. !!
YOU, !! GET IN FRONT OF THE ! CHIMNEY AND TELL ME IF SOMETHING COMES DOWN, !!
ALL RIGHT.
!! I CAN FEEL SOMETHING!
CAN'T YOU SEE ANYTHING COME OUT DOWN THERE? !!
FILTHY !! BIRDS!! IT'S ALL ROTTEN HERE! !
NO, STILL NOTHING!... HUH? YES, LOOKS LIKE...
WELL? !! IS IT OUT OR NOT?
YES!
BROMBROMBOM
805B

Blind Man's bluff

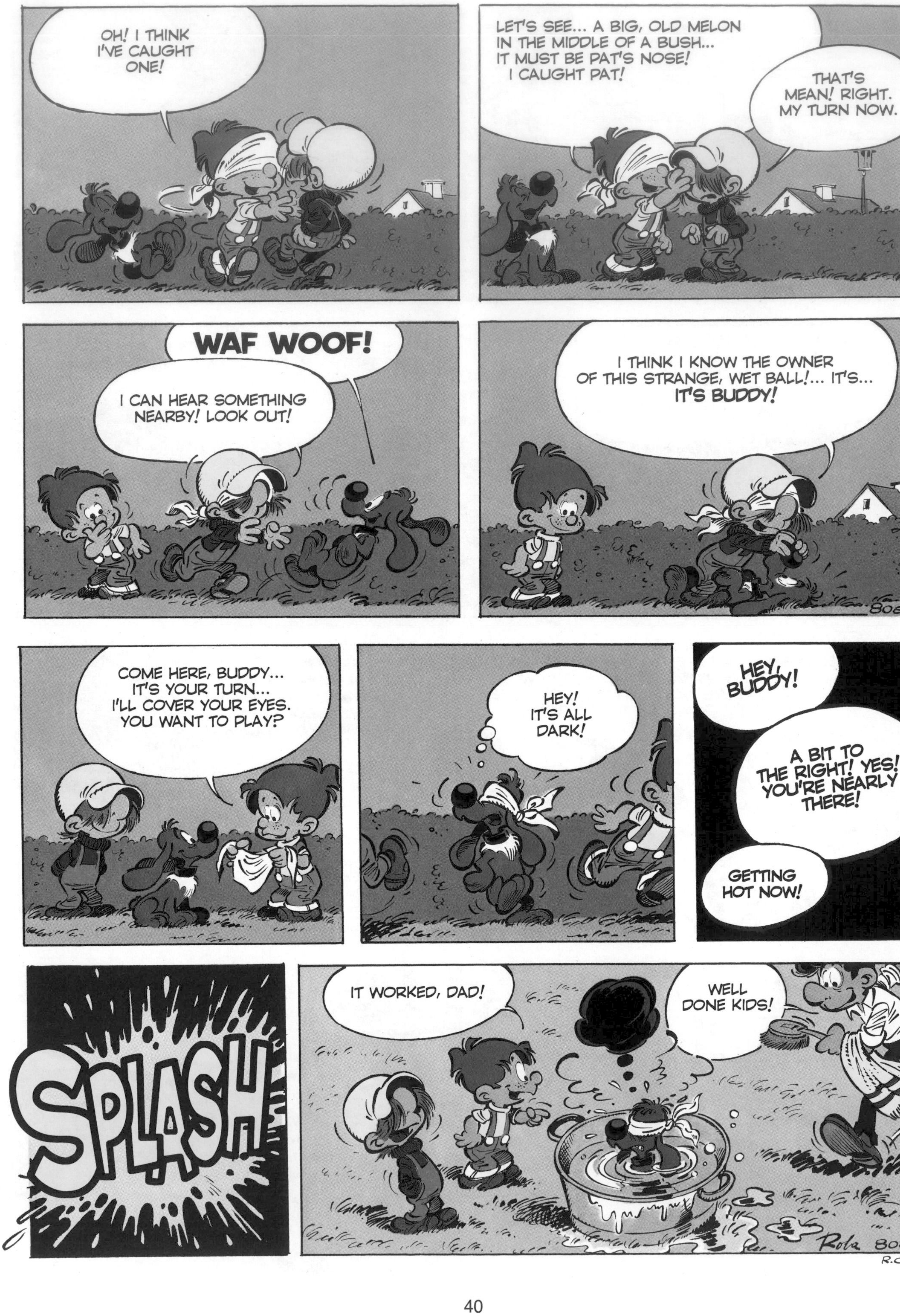
OH! I THINK I'VE CAUGHT ONE!
LET'S SEE... A BIG, OLD MELON IN THE MIDDLE OF A BUSH... IT MUST BE PAT'S NOSE! I CAUGHT PAT!
THAT'S MEAN! RIGHT. MY TURN NOW.
WAF WOOF!
I CAN HEAR SOMETHING NEARBY! LOOK OUT!
I THINK I KNOW THE OWNER OF THIS STRANGE, WET BALL!... IT'S... IT'S BUDDY!
806A
COME HERE, BUDDY... IT'S YOUR TURN... I'LL COVER YOUR EYES. YOU WANT TO PLAY?
HEY! IT'S ALL DARK!
HEY, BUDDY!
A BIT TO THE RIGHT! YES! YOU'RE NEARLY THERE!
GETTING HOT NOW!
SPLASH
IT WORKED, DAD!
WELL DONE KIDS!
Roba 806B
R.C.

What a Pickle!

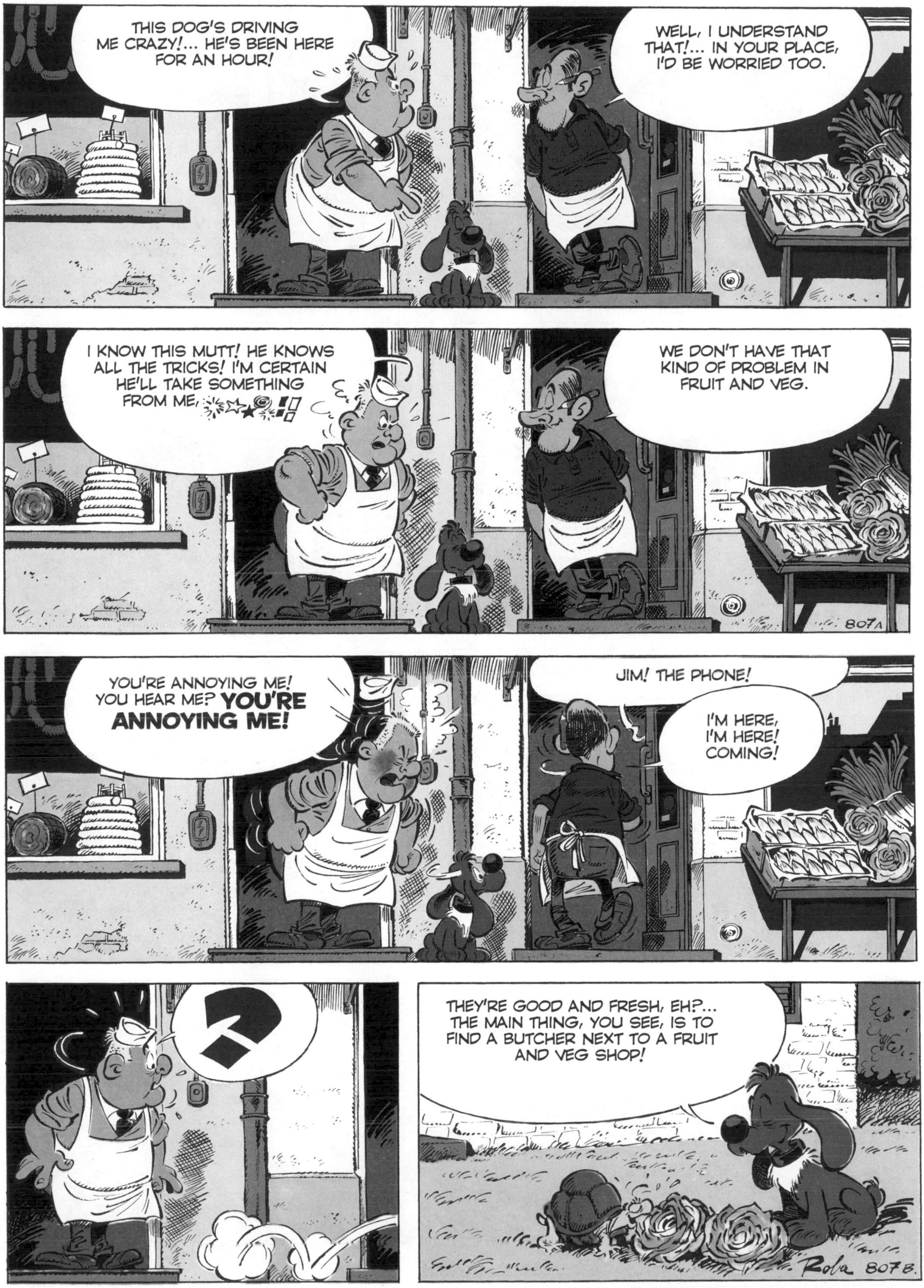

THIS DOG'S DRIVING ME CRAZY!... HE'S BEEN HERE FOR AN HOUR!
WELL, I UNDERSTAND THAT!... IN YOUR PLACE, I'D BE WORRIED TOO.
I KNOW THIS MUTT! HE KNOWS ALL THE TRICKS! I'M CERTAIN HE'LL TAKE SOMETHING FROM ME, !!
WE DON'T HAVE THAT KIND OF PROBLEM IN FRUIT AND VEG.
807A
YOU'RE ANNOYING ME! YOU HEAR ME? YOU'RE ANNOYING ME!
JIM! THE PHONE!
I'M HERE, I'M HERE! COMING!
?
THEY'RE GOOD AND FRESH, EH?... THE MAIN THING, YOU SEE, IS TO FIND A BUTCHER NEXT TO A FRUIT AND VEG SHOP!
Roba 807B.

A Little Click...

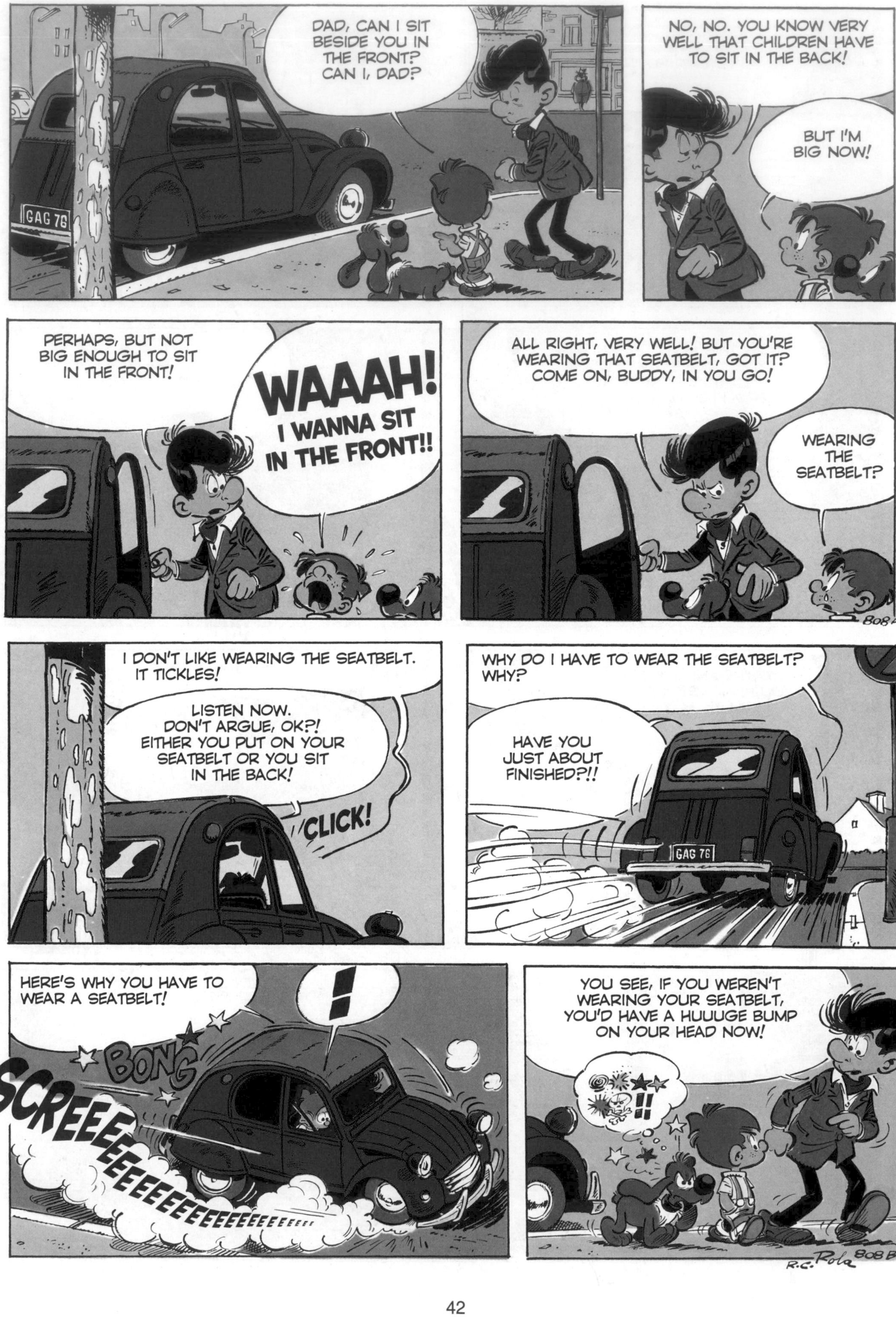

DAD, CAN I SIT BESIDE YOU IN THE FRONT? CAN I, DAD?
NO, NO. YOU KNOW VERY WELL THAT CHILDREN HAVE TO SIT IN THE BACK!
BUT I'M BIG NOW!
PERHAPS, BUT NOT BIG ENOUGH TO SIT IN THE FRONT!
WAAAH! I WANNA SIT IN THE FRONT!!
ALL RIGHT, VERY WELL! BUT YOU'RE WEARING THAT SEATBELT, GOT IT? COME ON, BUDDY, IN YOU GO!
WEARING THE SEATBELT?
I DON'T LIKE WEARING THE SEATBELT. IT TICKLES!
LISTEN NOW. DON'T ARGUE, OK?! EITHER YOU PUT ON YOUR SEATBELT OR YOU SIT IN THE BACK!
CLICK!
WHY DO I HAVE TO WEAR THE SEATBELT? WHY?
HAVE YOU JUST ABOUT FINISHED?!!
GAG 76
HERE'S WHY YOU HAVE TO WEAR A SEATBELT!
!
BONG
SCREEEEEEEEEEEEEEEEEEEE
YOU SEE, IF YOU WEREN'T WEARING YOUR SEATBELT, YOU'D HAVE A HUUUGE BUMP ON YOUR HEAD NOW!
!!

Rag Tag

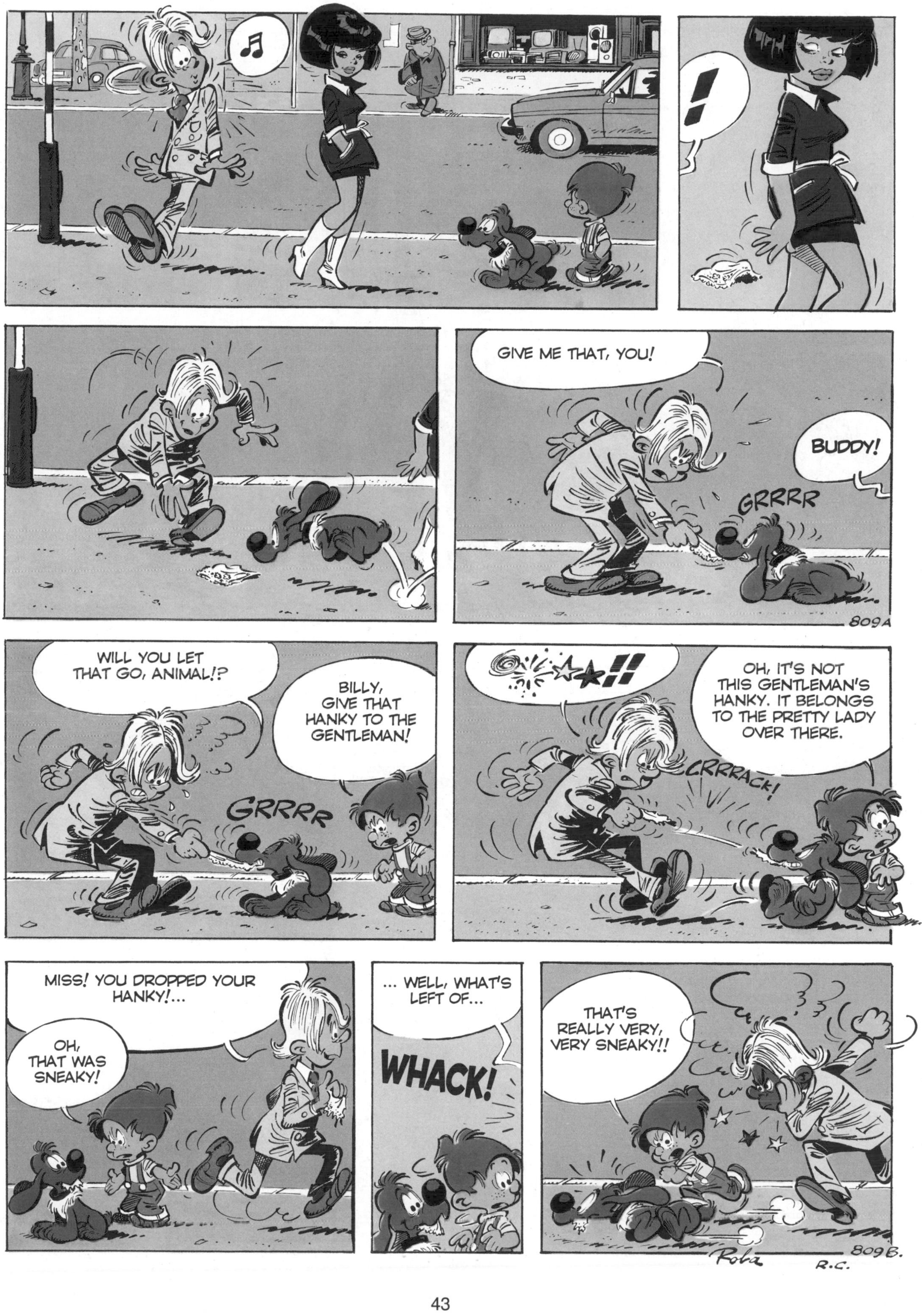

!
GIVE ME THAT, YOU!
BUDDY!
GRRRR
WILL YOU LET THAT GO, ANIMAL!?
GRRRR
BILLY, GIVE THAT HANKY TO THE GENTLEMAN!
OH, IT'S NOT THIS GENTLEMAN'S HANKY. IT BELONGS TO THE PRETTY LADY OVER THERE.
CRRRACK!
809A
MISS! YOU DROPPED YOUR HANKY!...
OH, THAT WAS SNEAKY!
... WELL, WHAT'S LEFT OF...
WHACK!
THAT'S REALLY VERY, VERY SNEAKY!!
809B.
Roba
R.C.

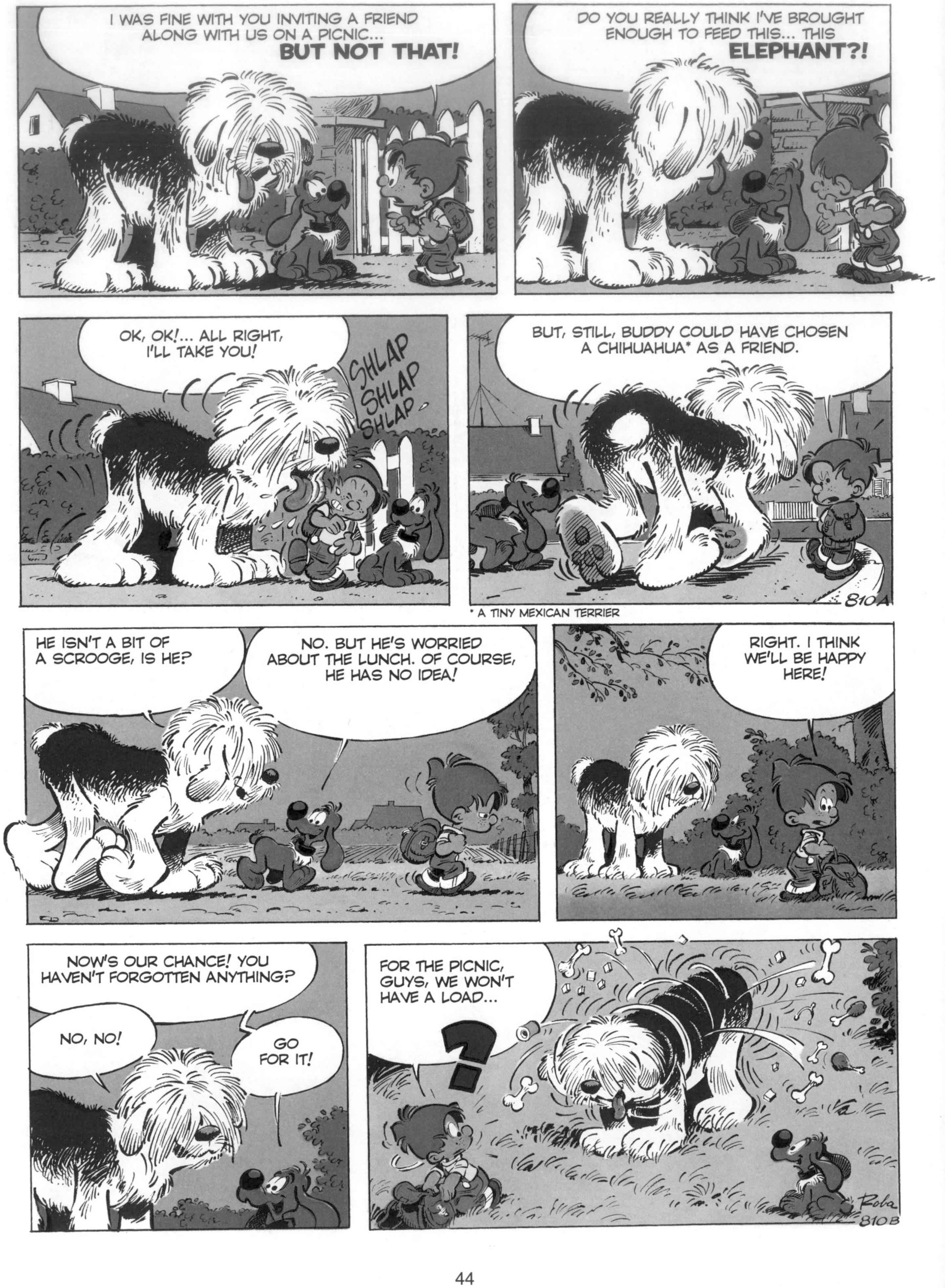
I WAS FINE WITH YOU INVITING A FRIEND ALONG WITH US ON A PICNIC... BUT NOT THAT!
DO YOU REALLY THINK I'VE BROUGHT ENOUGH TO FEED THIS... THIS ELEPHANT?!
OK, OK!... ALL RIGHT, I'LL TAKE YOU!
SHLAP SHLAP SHLAP
BUT, STILL, BUDDY COULD HAVE CHOSEN A CHIHUAHUA* AS A FRIEND.
810 A
* A TINY MEXICAN TERRIER
HE ISN'T A BIT OF A SCROOGE, IS HE?
NO. BUT HE'S WORRIED ABOUT THE LUNCH. OF COURSE, HE HAS NO IDEA!
RIGHT. I THINK WE'LL BE HAPPY HERE!
NOW'S OUR CHANCE! YOU HAVEN'T FORGOTTEN ANYTHING?
NO, NO!
GO FOR IT!
FOR THE PICNIC, GUYS, WE WON'T HAVE A LOAD...
?
Roba
810 B

Friends of the Forest

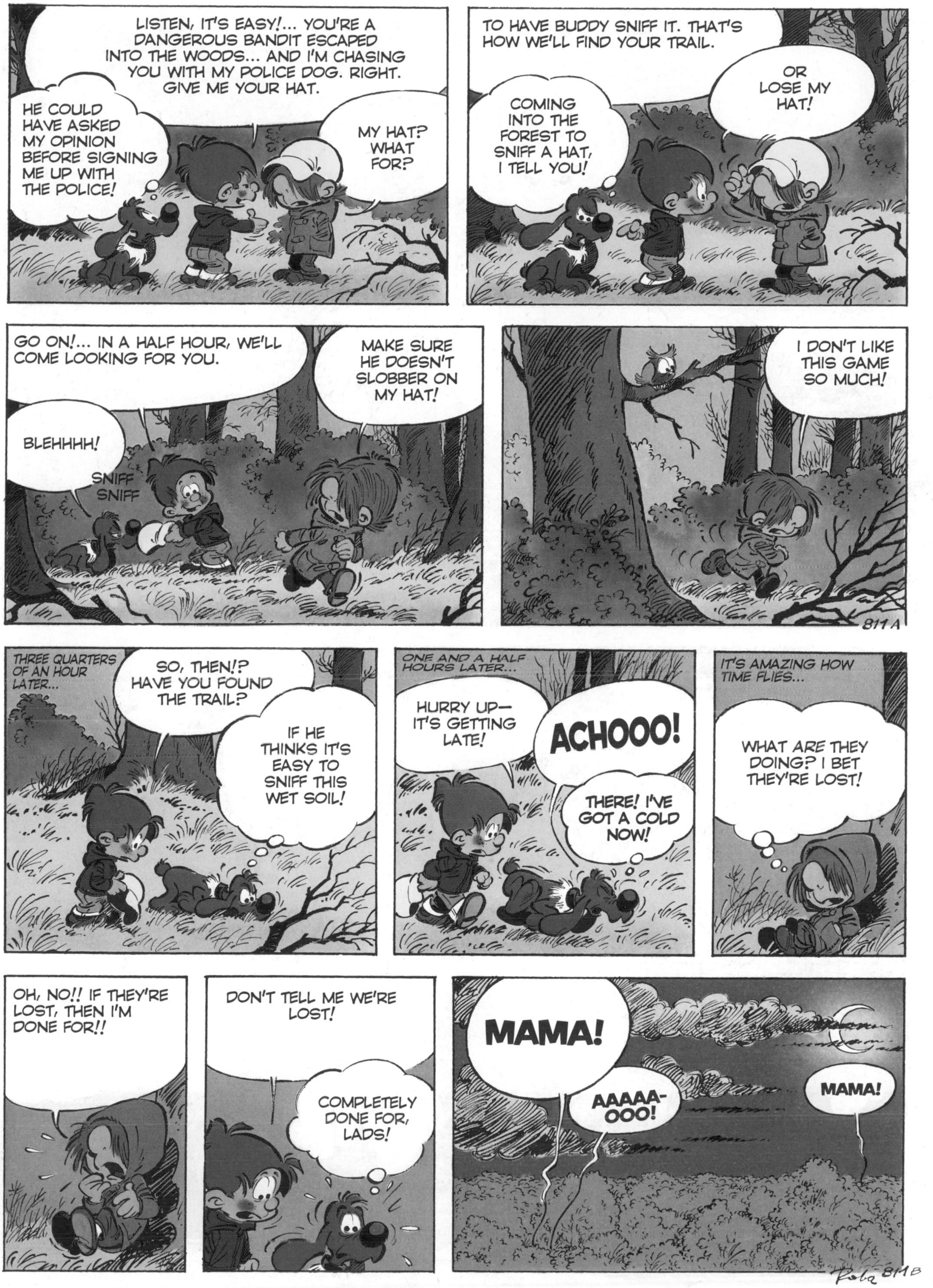

LISTEN, IT'S EASY!... YOU'RE A DANGEROUS BANDIT ESCAPED INTO THE WOODS... AND I'M CHASING YOU WITH MY POLICE DOG. RIGHT. GIVE ME YOUR HAT.
HE COULD HAVE ASKED MY OPINION BEFORE SIGNING ME UP WITH THE POLICE!
MY HAT? WHAT FOR?
TO HAVE BUDDY SNIFF IT. THAT'S HOW WE'LL FIND YOUR TRAIL.
COMING INTO THE FOREST TO SNIFF A HAT, I TELL YOU!
OR LOSE MY HAT!
GO ON!... IN A HALF HOUR, WE'LL COME LOOKING FOR YOU.
MAKE SURE HE DOESN'T SLOBBER ON MY HAT!
BLEHHHH!
SNIFF SNIFF
I DON'T LIKE THIS GAME SO MUCH!
811 A
THREE QUARTERS OF AN HOUR LATER...
SO, THEN!? HAVE YOU FOUND THE TRAIL?
IF HE THINKS IT'S EASY TO SNIFF THIS WET SOIL!
ONE AND A HALF HOURS LATER...
HURRY UP— IT'S GETTING LATE!
ACHOOO!
THERE! I'VE GOT A COLD NOW!
IT'S AMAZING HOW TIME FLIES...
WHAT ARE THEY DOING? I BET THEY'RE LOST!
OH, NO!! IF THEY'RE LOST, THEN I'M DONE FOR!!
DON'T TELL ME WE'RE LOST!
COMPLETELY DONE FOR, LADS!
MAMA!
AAAAA-OOO!
MAMA!
Roba 811 B

Very, Very Old Gag

BILLY!
IGNORAMUS!!
?
DON'T YOU REALISE HOW DANGEROUS IT IS TO THROW A BANANA SKIN AWAY LIKE YOU JUST DID?
I KNOW IT'S A GAG THAT HAS MADE MILLIONS OF PEOPLE LAUGH IN MOVIES AND COMICS, BUT STILL!
812 A
WHEN IT'S SO SIMPLE TO POP THIS SKIN IN THE BIN!
TO AVOID ACCIDENTS, YOU'LL DO THE SAME FROM NOW ON!... DO YOU UNDERSTAND?
YES, DAD.
ZZWIP
IF THERE'S ONE THING I HATE, IT'S PEOPLE THROWING BANANA SKINS INTO THE BIN I'M IN!
Roba 812B.

Billy & Buddy

1
Billy & Buddy
REMEMBER THIS, BUDDY?
CINEBOOK

2
Billy & Buddy
BORED SILLY WITH BILLY
CINEBOOK

3
Billy & Buddy
FRIENDS FIRST
CINEBOOK

4
Billy & Buddy
IT'S A DOG'S LIFE
CINEBOOK

5
Billy & Buddy
CLOWNING AROUND
CINEBOOK

6
Billy & Buddy
BUDDY'S GANG
CINEBOOK

7
Billy & Buddy
BEWARE OF (FUNNY) DOG!
CINEBOOK

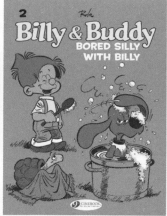

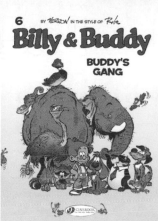

Billy & Buddy

COMING SOON

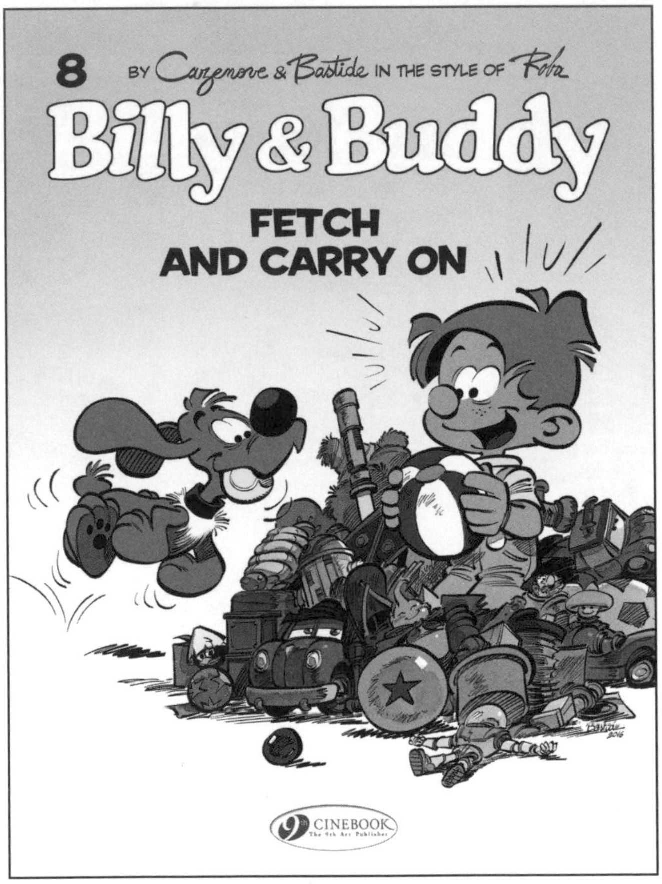
8
BY Cazenove & Bastide IN THE STYLE OF Roba
Billy & Buddy
FETCH
AND CARRY ON
CINEBOOK
The 9th Art Publisher